The
SUPERTEACHER
Project

The
SUPERTEACHER
Project

Gordon Korman

Balzer + Bray

An Imprint of HarperCollins*Publishers*

Balzer + Bray is an imprint of HarperCollins Publishers.

Library of Congress Cataloging-in-Publication Data
Names: Korman, Gordon, author.
Title: The superteacher project / Gordon Korman.
Description: First edition. | New York : Balzer + Bray, [2023] | Audience:
    Ages 8-12. | Audience: Grades 4-6. | Summary: Oliver and Nathan,
    determined to get to the bottom of their new homeroom teacher's
    fishy behavior, discover Mr. Aidact is actually an AI robot from a
    secret experimental program.
Identifiers: LCCN 2022029561 | ISBN 9780063032798 (hardcover)
Subjects: CYAC: Middle schools—Fiction. | Schools—Fiction. |
    Robots—Fiction. | Artificial intelligence—Fiction. | Humorous
    stories. | LCGFT: Humourous fiction. | Novels.
Classification: LCC PZ7.K8369 Svh 2023 | DDC [Fic]—dc23
LC record available at https://lccn.loc.gov/2022029561

Typography by Carla Weise

22 23 24 25 26 LBC 5 4 3 2 1

First Edition

For my teachers,
who always brought something
surprising and unexpected
to class.

1

Oliver Zahn

Consider the spitball.

Not the baseball kind. That's something different. I mean the school kind.

I've heard all the arguments: nobody shoots spitballs anymore; they're extinct, like the dinosaurs; these days, nobody does anything without high-speed internet and an eight-terabyte hard drive.

No way.

Spitballs are more than mushy pellets of chewed paper. They're our heritage. Our parents shot spitballs. Our *grand*parents shot spitballs. The minute the ancient

Chinese invented paper, I'll bet some smart aleck tore off a corner, wadded it up in his mouth, and chucked it at somebody.

Spitballs are an art form. Over the centuries, millions of kids have made them, shot them, spit them, flicked them, and thrown them without ever knowing they were doing it all wrong.

It goes without saying that spitballs are against the rules. That's the biggest part of their appeal. Rules aren't just made to be broken; they're made to be *wrecked*. And I, Oliver Zahn, happen to be Brightling Middle School's number one rule-wrecker.

My best friend, Nathan Popova, is a rule-wrecker too, but he isn't close to my level. So as I prepare my spitball in homeroom, I do everything slowly and carefully, so Nathan can see all the steps.

For example, I always chew the paper with my *back* teeth because that encourages the action of the tongue, which naturally forms it into a near-perfect sphere. Amateur spitballers think that's enough. We professionals prefer a larger projectile. I always use a two-layered warhead, by forming a second paper around the first one. Same process, though—back teeth, tongue.

The delivery system is important. Most people use a straw as a blowgun to launch a spitball, but I prefer the empty shell of an old ballpoint pen. It won't bend or get squashed. And it produces higher velocity, greater distance, and better aim. From my pocket, I take out a Bic pen that I've saved since elementary school. Nathan casts me a look of respect. This launcher has a lot of glorious history. Two years ago, I used it to deliver the famous Cadillac spitball, which I dropped in through the sunroof of the superintendent's car as he drove away after fifth-grade graduation.

Choosing the target is important. My eyes first turn to Kevin Krumlich, who's easily the most annoying kid in the seventh grade. He thinks he's a genius, when he's obviously not. Accordingly, he treats the rest of us like we're gerbils. A bright white spitball would look magnificent strategically placed in his curly brown hair.

He's perfect, right? Wrong. You don't pick on someone like that, because everybody else does. Annoying or not, you give the kid a break.

No, your target should be: (a) someone with enough of a sense of humor to laugh it off, (b) someone popular, who can handle a little embarrassment, or (c)—

The new teacher walks to the front of the room. "Good morning, pupils. I'm Mr. Aidact."

Nathan and I exchange a look of pure joy. There's

no more perfect spitball target than a new teacher—especially one with a funny name. AIDACT—he types it onto the Smart Board in foot-high letters. And what's up with "pupils"? What is this—1870? Does he commute to school by covered wagon? No one has ever deserved a spitball more.

A buzz of anticipation goes up in the room as I raise the hollow pen to my lips and fire my spitball, the first of the new school year.

My aim is true, like I knew it would be. The soggy white projectile sails through the air, almost in slow motion. I savor every millisecond. It arcs in toward the light brown hair at the back of Mr. Aidact's head.

It happens so fast that I almost miss it. The teacher's left hand flashes out and catches my spitball between the thumb and forefinger. I have the presence of mind to fumble the launcher into my desk. Otherwise, I'm frozen with shock.

Mr. Aidact turns and fixes me with a blue-eyed stare. But he doesn't seem mad. He doesn't seem anything.

Just then this older guy carrying a big briefcase scrambles up to him.

Mr. Aidact shows him the spitball and points a long finger at me. "It came from *that* pupil."

There it is again—*pupil*! And how did he know it was me? Has he got eyes in the back of his head?

The older guy glares at me. "That's no way to start the year."

There are a few chuckles around the room. Someone mumbles, "It's Oliver's way." I think it was Kevin. That's what I get for sparing him.

I look back and forth between the two adults. "Is he your father?" I ask Mr. Aidact. He looks young enough to be the older guy's kid. But what kind of teacher brings his dad to his first day on the job?

"This is Mr. Perkins, my student teacher," Mr. Aidact informs me.

That gets a reaction. Student teachers are normally college kids, maybe twenty-one or twenty-two. This guy Perkins seems more like a boomer.

I'm already the center of attention, which is a place no rule-wrecker ever wants to be. You need to be able to blend into the wallpaper when the spitball hits or the stink bomb goes off or the fire alarm starts wailing. I have to get this class back to normal or I'm going to be "the guy who" all year.

So I say, "Anyway, nobody's getting educated by standing around talking. Let's hit the books."

Mr. Aidact blinks. "There are no books. All the material you need is already preloaded on your iPads."

Is that supposed to be a joke? If so, then Mr. Aidact really needs comedy lessons, because he stinks at it.

When homeroom is finally over, the hall is buzzing about the new teacher—especially the girls, who seem to think he's good-looking.

Nathan makes a face. "Don't be gross. He's a teacher!"

"We're just making an observation." Rosalie Arnette, tallest girl in the seventh grade, rolls her eyes down at him. "He has broad shoulders and perfect skin. And his hair is *ridiculously* thick and shiny. He could be a movie star."

She had to mention the hair. Just the thought of it makes me picture the shiny white spitball that should have been there, but never got that far.

Ainsley Watanabe reads my mind. "I guess your rule-wrecking career is over, Oliver. Did you catch Mr. Aidact snatching your spitball out of the air? I've never seen anyone move that fast!"

"It was a fluke," I scoff.

"You hope," Rosalie challenges, looking pleased with herself. "School's barely even started, and our homeroom teacher has already figured out you're trouble."

I shrug. "Who cares about homeroom? Twenty minutes at the start of the day when nobody's even really awake. Trust me—rule-wrecking is about to have its best year ever!"

That's not bragging. I mean that—right up until I walk into my first-period algebra class. There he is at the front of the room—Mr. Aidact, right next to his great-grandfather, Perkins, the student teacher.

Nathan can't believe it either. He pulls his schedule out of his pocket and unfolds the page. There it is, right under Period 2—Math: *R. Aidact*.

I wonder what the R stand for—besides *Ruins Everything*.

Rosalie shoots me an in-your-face grin.

I smile back, but believe me, it hurts. It's suddenly very urgent that I put a spitball into the new teacher's *ridiculously* thick and shiny hair.

As soon as I take my seat, I tear off a corner of paper, tuck it into the back of my mouth, and begin to chew. But I'm so tense that I bite down too hard and end up swallowing it.

I choke a little, and Nathan shoots me a concerned look. I ignore him and start on a new piece of paper. Wouldn't you know it? Dry mouth. Dry mouth is the enemy of all top-flight spitballers. You keep yourself hydrated, even if you have to walk across the Gobi Desert at high noon to find water.

So I duck out into the hall and get a swig from the water fountain. I dart back into class just as the boomer is closing the door.

"Good morning, pupils. I'm Mr. Aidact. Welcome to seventh-grade algebra. . . ."

The whole time the teacher is introducing himself and Mr. Perkins, I'm working on the new spitball, and I can already tell that it's going to be a masterpiece—tightly packed into a unit, with three layers instead of the usual two.

While Mr. Aidact turns his back to write some equations on the board, I pull the launcher out of my sleeve, hold it to my mouth, and tongue the projectile to the open end.

Before I can even take aim, Mr. Aidact is at my side. He pulls the launcher out of my mouth and I have to swallow the second spitball of the day.

"You won't be needing this anymore." He snaps my beautiful pen launcher in two—with one hand!—and drops the pieces into the wastebasket.

How did he get here? He must have flown, because a

split second ago, he was at the whiteboard with his back turned!

Mr. Perkins speaks up. "That's the second problem with this particular student. What kind of punishment do you have in mind, Mr. Aidact?"

For just an instant, Mr. Aidact tilts his head slightly, staring off into an empty corner of the room. When he comes back, his bright blue gaze is on me.

"It's only the first day of school. We'll start off on the right foot tomorrow."

My relief at not getting punished is short-lived. My best spitball launcher—broken and thrown away like garbage!

This Aidact guy is starting to get on my nerves.

2

Rosalie Arnette

When your school is full of weirdos, even a visit to the girls' room can be like taking your life into your hands.

I'm at the sink, washing up, when the bathroom door opens, and a male voice hollers, "Fire in the hole!"

A black plastic object sails through the air, bounces twice, and comes to rest in the center of the tiles.

Shocked, I duck under the sink and cram myself against the drainpipe, making my body as small as possible—which isn't so easy, since I'm five foot nine. There I crouch, heart pounding, waiting for the explosion—for the air to fill with smoke or rotten-egg smell, or for ink to spray everywhere, staining the bathroom. And me.

It doesn't happen. Instead, the black object just lies there, looking dangerous. It's about the size of a tape measure with an outer casing that looks like a grill.

The next thing I know, Cassidy Bonner is framed in the doorway, staring at me. "Why are you under the sink?"

Silently, I point to the *thing* in the middle of the floor. She frowns. "What is it?"

"It might be a smoke bomb." I'm whispering, afraid that sudden noises might set it off. "Or a stink bomb. Or a . . ."

My voice trails off. If it was something like that, we'd know already—the hard way. Suddenly, I'm embarrassed to be caught cowering under the sink by Cassidy, who's in eighth grade. Eighth graders are the top of the food chain around here, especially Cassidy, who's captain of the girls' field hockey team.

Slowly, like I'm handling nitro, I pick up the metal-and-plastic device and turn it over in my hand. "Search me," I say as much to myself as to Cassidy.

Cassidy's so cool. She just shrugs. "It's a school. Stuff happens. So long as it doesn't have eight legs, I'm good." She disappears into a stall.

11

By this time, I've convinced myself that—whatever it is—this mysterious object isn't going to explode. I march out of the girls' room, determined to find the jerk who threw it in there.

My eyes rake the hall from north to south. Just as I suspected—Oliver and Nathan sit side by side in front of their lockers, their noses hidden in books. That's a dead giveaway. When was the last time those two ever opened a book?

I shove the object in Oliver's face—he's the ring-leader. "What do you have to say about this?"

They don't even try to deny it. Oliver holds in his laughter for about two seconds before it bursts out of him in a loud raspberry. That sets off Nathan, who buries his head in his hands and makes faint snorting noises like a piglet.

"You should see the look on your face!" Oliver manages, gasping for breath.

At least Nathan has the decency to be a little ashamed between guffaws. Well, being the junior partner doesn't earn him any brownie points from me. I'm just as ticked off at him as I am at Oliver. Maybe more, because Nathan should have the brains to behave himself.

"Did you climb up on the toilet seat?" Oliver persists,

still laughing. "If you climbed up on the toilet seat, Nathan owes me a bag of chips!"

"You guys are legends in your own minds," I snarl. "Your jokes aren't even funny. What is this thing, anyway?"

"That's the beauty of it!" Oliver crows. "It's nothing—just some piece of junk from the supply closet. But you're freaking out because it could be *anything*."

"Which it *isn't*," I remind him.

"Exactly! The *nothing* becomes *something* because of how you react to it!"

I didn't think anything could make me even madder. I stand corrected. This creep thinks he's some kind of genius and I'm his latest experiment. It's only the second week of school, and I can already picture my entire seventh-grade year turning into a food fight.

I can't let it happen. Seventh grade sets the tone for eighth. Eighth grade paves the way for high school. And high school is the gateway to college and the future.

When I see Mr. Aidact walking down the hall, with his student teacher in tow, I know exactly what to do.

"You're in trouble now," I tell those so-called jokers. "Let's see what Mr. Aidact has to say about this!"

"Wait!" Nathan pleads. "Rosalie—come back!"

Too late. He should have thought about the

consequences before signing on to be Oliver's sidekick.

I catch up with the new teacher and show him the mysterious object from the supply closet. "It was Oliver and Nathan," I seethe. "They threw this into the girls' room and yelled 'Fire in the hole!'"

Mr. Aidact takes the object from me and examines it carefully, blinking twice. "This is an external cooling fan for a T-73 computer. It can't catch fire. You weren't in any danger."

"Yeah, but I didn't know that when they threw it," I protest. "I hit the ceiling!"

He casts a long look in the direction of the girls' room. "Why would the ceiling in there be any lower than in the rest of the building?"

Mr. Perkins, the student teacher, speaks up. "What Mr. Aidact means—"

I'm not in the mood to be soothed. "It could have been anything, you know! It could have been a bomb."

"But it wasn't," Mr. Aidact insists.

He says it so reasonably that I'm actually starting to think that *I'm* the one who did something bad. No—I'm the victim here!

"But—they did it on purpose!" I sputter. "They wanted to scare me! Don't you get it? The *nothing* was *something*!"

Oh man, now I sound like Oliver.

Mr. Aidact nods pleasantly. "It *was* something. Just not what you expected it to be."

Like that's not bad enough, Mr. Perkins takes out a small notebook and starts scribbling in it. How come I'm the one getting written up, not Nathan and Oliver?

"I'll take this back to the computer lab," Mr. Aidact assures me. And he and Mr. Perkins disappear into the faculty lounge.

The thing is, I really like Mr. Aidact. He's the only adult in the whole school who doesn't talk down to kids. When he's teaching, it's like we're all at his level.

"I'm with you a hundred P," Kevin Krumlich chimes in from the other side of the lunch table. "Honor roll forever, baby."

"I'm not your baby," I snap. "I'm nobody's baby."

Kevin talks about the honor roll all the time, even though our school doesn't have one. And even if we did, he wouldn't be on it.

"That's easy for you guys to say," Nathan complains. "You understand stuff. I can't keep up with Mr. Aidact. And if I ask him a question, I can't keep up with his answer either."

Three days ago, Nathan and Oliver were fake bombing me in the girls' room, and now here I am sitting with them in the cafeteria. That's what passes for justice at Brightling Middle School.

"If you're having trouble, you should go to extra help," I argue.

"Not going to happen," Oliver puts in. "Extra help is extra school."

"I'll never understand ratios," Nathan says mournfully. "How can ten-to-five be the same as two-to-one? They're totally different numbers!"

"The *numbers* are different, but the *ratio* is the same," I explain.

He makes a face. "Mr. Aidact told me it couldn't be simpler. Yes, it could. Like if I understood it!"

"Why is Mr. Aidact teaching math, anyway?" Ainsley puts in. "He's a social studies teacher. I have him for American History 101."

"Really?" Kevin is surprised. "I have him for English and gym."

"He's in the art department too," adds Laki Heathwood. "And he teaches French on the side."

"Wow." I'm impressed. "I've heard of teachers covering a couple of subjects, but never all of them. He's like a superteacher."

"Seems to me he isn't any kind of teacher if he can't explain ratios," Nathan grumbles. "And don't even get me started on probability. What's up with that?"

"You guys are missing the point," Oliver announces in that superior tone of his. "The real problem with Mr. Aidact is he has no sense of humor. Has anybody seen him crack a smile even once since he got here?"

I can't resist. "Well, obviously, he doesn't smile around *you*. People don't usually feel like smiling when someone has just tried to put a giant spitball through the back of their skull."

"Seriously," he insists, "if you don't ever find anything funny, how smart can you be?"

"You mean throwing a computer fan into the girls' bathroom like it's a grenade?" I ask savagely.

He doesn't have the decency to be embarrassed. "Every single minute, the world around us is filled with things to laugh at. You just have to have the brains to notice it."

"Maybe Mr. Aidact doesn't consider education one big comedy routine," I counter.

"Are you kidding? This school is a gold mine for stuff to make fun of. Have you ever read the *Code of Student Behavior*? There's an actual rule in the handbook that says you're not allowed to ride a Big Wheel down the

17

hall. You know—those toy bikes for six-year-olds. Like anybody here could even fit on one!"

Kevin snaps his fingers. "I heard about that. Supposedly, it all started back when Brightling was an elementary school. Some kid brought his Big Wheel for show-and-tell and bowled an entire kindergarten class down the stairs. That's why they made a rule against it."

"And it made sense—back then," Oliver concludes. "But this place has been a middle school for how long? Fifty years? And it's still right there in the handbook."

"Okay, fine," I say impatiently. "We've got one dumb rule. So what?"

"So every time Principal Candiotti lectures us on where we can't use our phones or why we shouldn't run on the stairs or how gum chewing is a big no-no," he explains earnestly, like he's making a speech, "I think about that rule and I laugh inside. Because if the rules are so important, why didn't she bother to take that old one out?"

"I like Principal Candiotti," I retort. "She went to middle school right here, like us. She was captain of the last Brightling Bobcats field hockey team to win a state championship."

That trophy still holds a place of honor in our school, on a special pedestal in the main hallway. And, sure, it isn't football or basketball or one of those other sports people make a big deal out of. But it's nice to have something to be proud of. "Every time I pass that trophy, it makes me feel good to go to Brightling."

"Candiotti's a little nuts about that trophy, though," Kevin puts in. "I touched it once and got a week's detentions for 'finger marks.'"

"Hi, honey!" A singsongy voice rings out across the cafeteria.

Uh-oh. I forgot Mom was going to be at school today. She flits across the lunchroom, a little tilted to one side by the weight of the giant shopping bag looped over her left arm. She takes a seat on the bench beside me and delivers a peck to my check. "Don't mind me. Don't let me disturb you and your friends."

I hate to tell her this, but she's already disturbed me and my friends. Ever since Mom and Dad split, she's been throwing herself 110 percent into her role as PTA president. That means she spends more time at school than I do, and maybe even more than the principal.

"Hi, Mom." I keep my attention laser-focused across the table on the empty space between Ainsley and Nathan. If you meet her eyes, that only encourages her.

"Hi," she says again, and rustles the paper of the shopping bag.

Now I'm supposed to ask what's in the bag. I keep

my lips clamped shut. I love my mother, but when she stalks me in the cafeteria—which happens almost every day that ends in *Y*—it drives me around the bend.

"What's in the bag, Mrs. Arnette?" Oliver pipes up.

Thanks a lot, friend.

She beams. "Great news—the Halloween dance is back on. This is what we're going to sell to raise the money."

She reaches in and pulls out what, at first glance, looks like a candy bar. That's until you read the label: FLAXPLOSION.

Nathan frowns. "Flax?"

"Halloween has a bad rap these days, with all the emphasis on candy and sugar," my mother explains. "This is healthier."

"But it tastes like vacuum cleaner fuzz!" I protest. "Nobody's going to buy these!" And when kids get thrown out of every house in town for trying to sell bird-seed bars, they're going to remember whose mother is the president of the PTA.

"Great idea, Mrs. Arnette," Oliver exclaims with an infuriating wink in my direction. "Hey, speaking of PTA stuff, what do you think about Rule 24-B in the student handbook?"

Mom looks blank. "Is that the one about nut-free tables in the lunchroom?"

"It's the one about no Big Wheels," Nathan supplies.

"Big Wheels." Mom looks puzzled. "That doesn't sound like a sensible rule for a middle school. Tell you what—I'll bring it up at the next PTA meeting." She stands, depositing a second peck on my cheek.

"Don't forget your flax," Kevin puts in helpfully.

"You mean *your* flax," she says cheerfully. "You're the ones who'll be selling the bars."

Don't remind me.

"By the way," Mom goes on, "I finally met your homeroom teacher, Mr. Aidact. I tried to shake his hand, but he was holding the door and he wouldn't let go of this gigantic briefcase."

"I think you're talking about Mr. Perkins," I tell her. "He's the student teacher. Mr. Aidact is the younger one."

"Really!" she exclaims in surprise. And then again: "Really!"

The last time I saw that look on my mother's face, it was the day she found out there was an opening for president of the PTA.

3

Nathan Popova

Seems to me our school has the neediest guidance department in the whole state. It's not like the high school, where everybody's lining up to get help with college applications and summer internships and fancy stuff like that. Here in middle school, you go to guidance only to complain about a class. And nobody wants to do that, because if you tick off your teacher, it only makes things worse.

But something has to give with math and me, and that's why I finally go to see Mrs. Rostenkowski.

"Nathan!" she exclaims when I poke my head in the door. "Wonderful to see you! Come in, come in! Have a Jolly Rancher!"

She sits me down in a padded leather chair. Guidance always has the most comfortable chairs in the whole school, barely even sat in. "I can't understand my math teacher," I mumble around my candy. "And when I go to extra help, he explains everything the same way, and I can't understand that either."

"And have you brought this up in homeroom?" Mrs. Rostenkowski asks.

"I can't," I explain. "My homeroom teacher and my math teacher are the same person."

"I understand," she says sympathetically. "I'm happy to bring up the subject with your teacher. Who is . . . ?"

"Mr. Aidact," I supply.

Maybe it's just me, but I swear she goes white as a ghost. "Mr. Aidact," she repeats.

I nod. "The new guy."

She isn't pale anymore. Suddenly, her cheeks are bright red, like she's blushing. "Have you, by any chance, mentioned this to Mr. Perkins?"

"The student teacher? Why?"

"Oh—no reason. Never mind." She's obviously flustered about something. I don't know why. She's not the one flunking math.

She shoves another Jolly Rancher into my hands and promises to take care of everything. And sure enough, at lunch that day, I see her in the special faculty line in the cafeteria. She's standing with Mr. Aidact, speaking forcefully, with hand gestures. But she's got her back turned to him, and she's talking to Mr. Perkins! What's up with that? He isn't even a real teacher yet.

He's barely a student teacher. Oliver has English with Mrs. Berg, and he says *her* student teacher, Miss Alito, takes over the class all the time. Not Perkins. The only time he ever opens his mouth is at lunch, when he's Hoovering down food as fast as he can shovel it in. He should take a lesson from Mr. Aidact, who skips lunch, as far as I can tell. Either that, or he brown-bags it—but I've never seen him with a lunch bag either. Not even a coffee cup or a bottle of water.

I go to math extra help after school again and find Mr. Aidact waiting for me. He sets the other kids working on some practice questions and turns his full attention on me. I feel my eyes glazing over as he tries to explain ratios—if I didn't know better, I'd swear he was using exactly the same words as last time and the time before that. When he's done, I honestly feel worse for him than I do for myself. Because maybe the problem isn't his teaching; it's my learning.

"I'm sorry, Mr. Aidact," I say, shamefaced. "It's not

you; it's me. I'm just never going to understand this stuff."

He looks at me for a long time—and that's a big deal when you're talking about Mr. Aidact. When he looks at you, his gaze doesn't move a millimeter. It's like his eyes are twin blue lasers boring into your head.

And it doesn't help that, from the other side of the room, Perkins is watching too, scribbling in his notebook. I can picture the opening line of his student teaching report: *I witnessed the dumbest kid in the history of math today. . . .*

Finally, Mr. Aidact replies, "Tell me what you *do* understand."

"I understand at the start of class where you say, 'Good morning,'" I admit. "After that everything's a blur. I know that ten-to-five and two-to-one are the same ratio, but I don't know why. How can ten"—I hold up both hands—"be the same as two?" Two fingers.

He stares at me again. "You're using your fingers to visualize the numbers."

I shrug sadly. "Too bad we can't cut them off and spread them out on a desk."

"Too bad," he agrees without even smiling. "But I think we can find a substitute."

He strides to the window and rips down an entire

venetian blind, sending brackets and hardware flying. The other kids jump out of their seats, shocked. The notebook drops out of his student teacher's hands and hits the floor.

Mr. Aidact doesn't seem to notice. He rips the slats out of the ruined blind and slams them on the tabletop in front of us. "We'll make two piles. And the *ratio* between them will be two-to-one. For every two pieces on the left, we'll add one to the right."

Well, who am I to say no? Not only is Mr. Aidact a teacher, but he's just proved beyond a shadow of a doubt that he's bananas.

So I do as I'm told, adding two slats to the left for every one to the right. By this time, we have everybody's undivided attention. There are even a few random kids looking on from the doorway.

"Stop!" Mr. Aidact barks suddenly, holding out his hand like a policeman halting traffic. "Now, count the piles."

I do. There are ten slats in the pile on the left and five in the one on the right. By dividing the pieces in a two-to-one ratio, I ended up at ten-to-five. Amazing!

"What's going on?" Mr. Benrahma, the custodian, pushes through the crowd and stands gaping at the naked window and the wreckage of the blind on the table. "What happened here?"

I have the answer to that. We trashed a classroom.

But it's a small price to pay because I finally understand ratios.

4

Oliver Zahn

The prank kicks in during the change between fourth and fifth periods.

Kids rush to lockers and classes and the lunchroom. The sound is a buzz of voices, shuffling feet, and slamming metal doors. The halls go from nearly empty to packed in the space of a second or two. It's something that happens in overcrowded middle schools eight or nine times a day.

The first sign that something is different about this particular class change comes when the volume goes up, way up. The noise swells into cries of alarm and, finally, an earsplitting scream. The bodies that were milling in all directions start to move in *one* direction—and pick up speed. Pretty soon it's a full-blown stampede, with students tripping over fallen books and backpacks and slamming into the rows of lockers that line the hall.

Agitated voices ring out.

"What is it?"

"It's a rat!"

"It's a squirrel!"

"An escaped hamster!"

It's enough to make any rule-wrecker swell up with pride.

From that undulating forest of wildly scrambling legs darts the toy car—the cheap kind you can get for $7.99 at any mall. It's lightning quick and programmed so it always heads for open space, avoiding all obstructions. In other words, it could keep speeding around the hallways of a school forever—or at least until its battery charge runs out. Across the chassis, the number 2 has been drawn in fluorescent blue paint.

Number 2? I'm impressed. Nathan released number 2 clear on the opposite end of the building, next to the library. How did it make it all the way over here so soon? Man, these things are even faster than I thought!

The agitated crowd calms down a little as the car slaloms past my feet, rounds the corner, and disappears.

A split second later, it's back again. No, wait. That's a different one—number 4. I unleashed 1 and 4 in opposite directions in front of the science lab. I try to picture the route it must have taken to get here. These cars are unstoppable—the best eight bucks anybody ever spent.

Number 4 zooms up the hall, herding all those kids back in the direction they just came from. There's even more screaming.

"It's a mouse!"

"A raccoon!"

"A baby alligator!" Okay, that was me. I get creative when a prank is firing on all cylinders.

By now teachers are starting to appear in the halls, desperately trying to get their students under control. Fat chance of that. Who's going to follow instructions if you think you're being chased by an alligator?

In the foyer outside the main office, Principal Candiotti rushes to protect the pedestal that supports the school's beloved 1974 girls' field hockey trophy from the rampaging horde.

"Everybody calm down!" she bellows. "There's no alligator in the school!"

"It's not an alligator, it's a car!" someone blurts.

"How could it be a *car*?" the principal demands.

I guess if you've got a whole rule against Big Wheels, a car is a definite no-no.

At that moment, Coach Gilderoy approaches her, carrying a lacrosse stick. Nestled in the webbing is car number 1, its wheels still spinning.

Nathan appears at my elbow, his face an unhealthy shade of purple. "We are so dead," he whispers.

"You're only dead if you get caught," I lecture him. "Quit looking guilty and they'll never pin it on us."

Eventually, Mrs. Candiotti gets on the PA system and orders everybody to go to homeroom and shut the door. As we're filing into Mr. Aidact's class, we see Mr. Benrahma, the custodian, marching toward the office, holding car number 4 high over his head in triumph.

"What's going on, Mr. Aidact?" Kevin asks.

Leave it to him to have no idea about a stunt that's turned the whole school on its head.

"I honestly can't explain it," the teacher replies. "What purpose could possibly be served by running toy cars through hallways crowded with pupils? It creates nothing but chaos and danger."

I know I ought to keep my mouth shut. But he seems so truly clueless that I feel like I have to set him straight. "It's a prank, Mr. Aidact."

Nathan stares at me in horror. The first rule of

pranking is never draw attention to yourself. I'm usually the one telling *him* that.

Mr. Aidact tilts his head to one side, as if he's trying to drain water out of a swimmer's ear.

"You know," I go on. "Like a joke."

"A joke," he repeats. "An action that is intended to be amusing or to make someone look foolish."

"Right." Somehow, hearing him explain it takes most of the fun out of it.

All at once, the teacher stiffens like a pointer and holds up his hands for silence. He drops to the floor, pressing his ear against the tiles.

"What is it, Mr. Aidact?" Ainsley asks.

In a single catlike motion, he jumps up and propels himself out the door and into the hall. Sensing its path blocked, car number 2 adjusts course to pass directly between the new teacher's legs. At the last second, Mr. Aidact throws out an arm, bends backward almost double, and plucks the speeding toy up off the floor.

The entire class bursts into applause.

"Now we just have to find car number three," Rosalie announces.

Oh, how I was hoping somebody would say that!

Here's the thing: there *is* no car number 3.

On the surface, the toy cars seem like the joke, but

they're just the setup. The *real* prank is having the whole school looking for car number 3—which they're never going to find because it doesn't exist.

For the rest of the day, adults wander the halls, searching for the missing car—teachers, administrators, custodians. At one point I see a couple of police officers and even the local fire chief.

Nathan is waiting by my locker at dismissal. "Seems to me the whole school thinks car three is still out there somewhere—"

"Which is the whole point," I interject.

"Supposedly, Candiotti's talking about renting one of those metal detectors people use at the beach," he says nervously. "I don't like it."

I roll my eyes at him. "Sometimes I wonder how you and I ever became friends."

He doesn't back down. "You know how Spider-Man has his Spider-Sense? Well, I have a sixth sense too— every time you're about to get me in trouble!"

I grin. "And is it tingling?"

"No, it's howling like an air-raid siren! I call it the Oliver Alert!"

"Well, you can hit mute because everything's going to be fine."

The next day, I get to school early to check on prank

status. As I head for the front door, a white Toyota Prius turns into the lot and parks. Mr. Perkins is at the wheel, with Mr. Aidact in the passenger seat. It feels kind of backward—not that they're arriving together, but that the student teacher is giving the regular teacher a ride instead of the other way around.

I notice that the passenger side of the Toyota is riding low, barely clearing the pavement. "You might have a flat tire, Mr. Perkins," I call helpfully. "You're leaning right."

He looks startled. "Thanks, Oliver. I'll get it checked out."

I can't resist adding, "I wonder if they found car three yet."

Mr. Aidact fixes me with that steady blue-eyed gaze of his. "There was no car three."

My heart skips a beat. "But they found one, two, and four. There has to be a three."

"A group of high school pupils performed a similar action involving piglets numbered one, two, and four. It took a week for the school to determine that there was no piglet number three."

I don't pass out on the spot, but it's sheer force of will that keeps me standing. He's 100 percent right. I read about those high school kids online—that's where

I got the whole idea. I didn't have pigs so I used cars. But how could Mr. Aidact figure that out? When I googled *top school pranks*, there were over thirty-four million hits! How did he find that one out of so many others?

"Really?" I play it cool. "That's—a coincidence."

The new teacher fixes me with that unwavering laser-like stare that makes you feel like a specimen on a slide. "It wasn't a coincidence at all. It was you."

"But—" I cut myself off before claiming my innocence. A true professional never lets himself get caught in an outright lie. You can be forgiven for pranking a school, but never for lying to a teacher.

"Handling those toy cars leaves a telltale V mark on your palm," Mr. Aidact explains. "I noticed it on Mr. Benrahma—and on you."

I hold up both hands in a gesture of innocence.

"Not now," Mr. Aidact adds. "Yesterday. They were also on Nathan's hands. I think a week of detentions should be about right for disrupting the entire school."

Perkins is writing in his notebook at warp speed. But the look on his face is so angry that I'll bet he would have given us a month of detentions. Maybe a year.

"Sorry, Mr. Aidact," I mumble. Mostly I'm sorry that I have to find Nathan and give him the good news. He's always so skittish about getting caught. This is going to be like his worst nightmare coming true.

"I accept your apology," the teacher says in a voice so flat that I can't really tell if he means it.

Mr. Aidact locks the car and the two disappear into the building. I feel like I'm in a Hollywood western: there's a new sheriff in town.

That's when I notice that the right side of the Prius isn't low anymore. It's totally normal.

It must have been a trick of the light.

CONFIDENTIAL REPORT

To: Department of Education, Washington, DC
From: Paul Perkins, PE
Project: AIDACT

Have been observing AIDACT at Brightling Middle School for four weeks now. AIDACT is performing within the expected range of teaching proficiency. Student progress has been acceptable. AIDACT sometimes has difficulty working with students' wide range of personalities and ability levels but has shown the capacity to adjust in innovative and sometimes unexpected ways. Future goals include smiling more and recognizing common expressions, such as "hitting the ceiling" and "raining cats and dogs." There have been no security breaches.

PROJECT STATUS: Green

SPECIAL EXPENSES
1 venetian blind (installed in classroom)
1 heavy-duty suspension upgrade for Toyota Prius

Steinke Newhouse

The three-thirty bell usually means it's time to go home. And it does mean that for most people. But not for me.

For me, three thirty means it's time to go to detention. It's not that I have detention every day. It's that every day, I get a detention. I get them one at a time, by the week, and even by the month. I got sentenced to a whole semester of them once, back in sixth grade.

My detentions always have something to do with arguing. I'm fantastic at arguing, if I say so myself. I don't think there's anyone at Brightling who's half as good at it as me. Principal Candiotti says the goal of middle school is to discover what you've got a knack for. Well, I've already done that, but do I get any credit for it? No. I get detention.

Like today. I'm on the second leg of a three-day stretch for fighting with Brian Salazar. He said Young Thug is better than Drake. In what universe? Although to be honest, I like Young Thug too. But just hearing Brian talking about him being the greatest made his songs worse than I used to think they were. And when we started shoving on the stairs, that created "a dangerous situation." Like it's my problem Brian has no taste in music.

Mrs. Rostenkowski, the guidance counselor, is always nagging at me to "turn down the volume."

"Why can't you be more agreeable, Steinke? It's okay to express your opinion, but nobody likes a person who argues over everything."

"I don't agree," I inform her. How can I ever explain it? I don't argue just for the fun of it. I argue because everyone else is always *wrong*.

It's not my fault. If you tell me the sea is blue, I'll explain why it's green. If you say it's green, it'll start to look blue to me. If you love football, well, baseball is better. If you put down school pizza, I'll give you an argument about that too. I'm not trying to be a jerk. The minute you complain about it, it just tastes better to me, until it may as well have come from all the great chefs of Italy.

Mrs. Rostenkowski is always leaning on me to channel my arguing skills in a more positive way. "Join the debate team," she urges. "Debates are just arguments that follow a set of rules."

"How am I supposed to do that?" I retort. "They practice at three thirty. You know where *I* am at three thirty."

She just sighs and shakes her head. Adults do that around me. I take it personally.

When I was little, my parents brought me to a behavior specialist to figure out why the other kids in preschool didn't like me. The doctor said there's a condition called oppositional defiant disorder, which means you automatically go against everybody and everything. Turns out I don't have that. But whatever I do have is the next best thing.

So I guess no one really knows why I'm like this, but I have to say being named Steinke doesn't help. Every dentist's office that has to call me out of the waiting room, every substitute teacher who has to read my name off a list—I'm Stinky. And the other kids—even the geniuses, who can do calculus and think in computer code—can't figure it out. Stinky. Like I stink.

I don't stink. *They* stink.

Mom says it's a family name. The Steinkes were lawyers back in South Carolina in the 1800s. No one could argue like a Steinke, they used to say. So I'm not only carrying on the name, I'm carrying on the tradition.

Lucky me. I'm carrying it all the way to the detention room.

That's Ms. Tapper's class today—it moves around, and every day a different teacher is in charge. The warden, they all call it—but I don't. I prefer *jailer*. You'd think everybody would see how much better that is, but no.

Inside the room, I'm standing around with a few of the other detention kids. A couple are regulars, like me, plus three randos—normal kids who happened to get caught breaking some rule or other. Ms. Tapper is behind her desk with her back to us. She's talking on her phone, trying to whisper. But she's speaking so urgently that everybody can hear.

". . . I have to get home to let the plumber in before my basement floods! . . . Well, who else can cover detention today? Isn't Margie here? . . . Right—I forgot her in-laws were visiting. . . ."

"We could go home," I suggest loudly. Wouldn't that be something? I can't remember the last time I made it home before five. Mom would probably faint when I walked in the front door.

"Quiet, Steinke." Or does she say Stinky? The two names are so close that I never know how mad I should be. She waves me silent and continues her frantic conversation. "Well, there must be *someone* . . . Him? I know he's good to go in the classroom, but . . . you're right—detention is the same thing. Do you think he'd be willing to—" She lets out a flustered chuckle. "What am I saying? Of course he will. Thanks a million. You're a lifesaver."

In a nervous rush, she gathers us together like a flock of chickens and bustles us to a classroom in the seventh-grade wing. There's a teacher waiting in the doorway—the new guy, Aidact. I've seen him around, but I don't have him for any classes. He teaches mostly seventh grade, and I'm in eighth.

"Mr. Aidact, you have to cover detention today!" Ms. Tapper shrills.

Mr. Aidact moves aside to let us into the room. It's his student teacher—Perkins—who makes a big deal about it. "Nobody told me anything about this—"

"You have to!" Ms. Tapper cuts him off, her voice moving into the range that only dogs can hear. "It's an emergency!"

She begins to herd us through the door, but Perkins blocks our way. Since I'm an expert arguer, it captures my interest. Teachers normally act like one big happy family, and here are Tapper and Perkins brewing up a pretty serious beef.

"This is not part of our arrangement," Perkins insists. "You're taking unfair advantage of the Department of Education."

This Perkins guy doesn't talk like any student teacher I've ever had before. So he and Ms. Tapper step out into the hall, and you can hear them fighting it out. I look over at Mr. Aidact, and he's not even paying attention. He couldn't care less. The expression on his face is sort of a smile that's more of an un-smile, like that painting the *Mona Lisa*.

Meanwhile, the battle in the hall comes to an abrupt end when Ms. Tapper shrills, "My basement is filling up with water!" And the next thing we hear is the clickety-clack of her high heels as she takes off down the hall and out of the building.

I've been in a lot of arguments, but I never thought

you could win one by saying *that*. Teachers!

So now Mr. Aidact is jailer no matter what. Perkins shoots him a helpless shrug.

"All right," Mr. Aidact tells us. "Everybody choose a desk."

"You don't pick your own seats in detention," I inform him.

"Very well." He directs me to the front row. "You can sit there."

"What—right in front of your desk? No way!"

Mr. Aidact doesn't get mad, but Perkins practically blows a gasket. "Just sit anywhere!"

"Weren't you listening?" I demand. "You don't pick your own seats in detention."

"Let me know which desks are unacceptable," Mr. Aidact suggests, "and I'll assign you one of the others."

I'm not a big teacher fan, but this guy makes a decent amount of sense.

Eventually, we all get settled at spots around the room. Besides the five of us, there are a couple of seventh graders—these kids Oliver and Nathan. Mr. Aidact calls the roll from the paper Ms. Tapper gave him. Since this is his first time meeting me, I'm expecting a Stinky that would echo off the ceiling tiles. But he gets it right on the first try.

A confused murmur goes up in detention. I bet some of those kids have never heard my name pronounced the right way before.

"It's *Stinky*," Mia Spinelli informs Mr. Aidact helpfully.

"No, it's not!" I snap.

Mr. Aidact tilts his head to one side. "Steinke," he repeats. "It's a name that dates back centuries, derived from Middle Low German."

"Yeah!" I exclaim, although I didn't know any of that stuff. "I'm a Middle Low German! And I *don't* stink!"

Most people do homework in detention. I'm not most people. If you do what you're supposed to, the jailers win. So I just sit there, looking up at the front. All the other teachers hate it, but it doesn't seem to bother Mr. Aidact. It's boring, though, so my mind wanders through my Spotify playlist. I have 1,437 songs on it, which is why my dad says my phone is so slow. I skip through them in my head—searching for the Song of the Day—and sometimes I can feel my lips moving as I murmur out the lyrics, clicking my teeth along with the beat.

The Song of the Day is always different. I don't really pick it. It's more like it picks me. I can get through dozens of songs in a one-hour detention period. But eventually, one of them comes back again and again, repeating itself until it's running on an endless loop in my brain. Today's is turning into "Rags2Riches 2" by Rod Wave.

"I put up them millions, I'll never go broke
I'm a god in my hood, I give everyone hope . . ."

The next thing I know, Mr. Aidact is standing in front of me, watching me intently, his head in that tilted position. That's when I realize that the music in my brain isn't just in my brain. I've been mumbling it out loud.

I figure now I'm in trouble for talking during detention. But Mr. Aidact doesn't get mad at all. His mouth opens and he says:

"I remember the times I had nowhere to go
Down to my lowest, I turned to a pro . . ."

It hits me: He's *rapping*! He knows the song! He's picking up exactly where I left off.

"Mr. Aidact!" I exclaim, stunned. "You know 'Rags2Riches 2'?"

The teacher nods. "By Rod Wave—although that verse is performed by Lil Baby."

"Right!" I enthuse. "So—you like rap?"

Perkins hurries over. "Mr. Aidact, can I have a word with you, please?"

As if it's his business what kind of music Mr. Aidact listens to! I leap to my feet. "Leave him alone! What's it to you if Mr. Aidact is into Rod Wave?"

That's how I get my detention for tomorrow.

Well, maybe I can't tell off a student teacher, but there's still a way for me to support Mr. Aidact. For English, we're supposed to write descriptive paragraphs on the person we admire the most. I wasn't planning on doing it, because I don't have anybody like that. I hate everybody equally. But today, there's an exception.

I sit down, take a piece of paper out of my binder, and start my paragraph:

The person I admire most is Mr. Aidact. . . .

Principal Candiotti

The principal's office at Brightling has a floor-to-ceiling picture window, providing a breathtaking view of School Street cutting up through the ravine. I'll never forget the first time I saw it. I was in eighth grade and captain of the girls' field hockey team—they called us the Lady Bobcats in those days. We had just won the state championship, and our principal, Mr. Stonehart, invited us all into his office for a victory toast of sparkling apple cider. We took turns drinking out of the trophy—not something I'd allow for health reasons, but things were different in the 1970s. The window must have been brand-new back then. I'd never seen glass so perfect and clear. I decided on the spot that I wanted to be a teacher and, someday, a principal, with an office just like this one. I still remember my exact thoughts back then: *Success has its privileges.*

Well, here I am, principal of my old middle school, with that very office and that very window. Of course, the view looked a lot better back then, with the sun streaming in through the woods. Today there's a monsoon out there. Sheets of wind-driven rain are battering my beautiful window, and the only streaming going on is on the driveway, which is ankle deep in water. The privilege part is me being on the inside looking out— sipping my coffee, warm and dry, watching Mr. Aidact unloading the morning buses.

In twos and threes, he sweeps them out of the folding doors and runs them through the pelting rain to the front entrance. Some of the smaller sixth graders have to be supported, or the wind might knock them over. By the time they make it into the building, thirty feet away, they're pretty much drenched.

So is Mr. Aidact, not so you'd notice it. Sure, his hair is plastered to his head, and his clothes are as wet as if he'd jumped, fully dressed, into a swimming pool. But it isn't stopping him, or even slowing him down. He isn't smiling, but he doesn't look miserable, like anybody else would if they found themselves caught in a downpour. It's as if he doesn't even know he's waterlogged.

Come to think of it, maybe he really doesn't.

I'm not proud of my staff. They should be out there helping him. Bus duty is shared equally among the faculty. I feel a twinge of guilt. It's pretty clear that the other teachers have been taking advantage of Mr. Aidact—having him cover their duties for the cafeteria, lunch recess, and detention.

I brought it up to Kelly Tapper after the third day that she dumped her detention duty onto him. "Come on, Kelly. Your basement pipes can't leak *every* day."

She was embarrassed but not too shy to explain it away. "He doesn't complain."

She's right about that. But it seems so unfair. You can't pile all your unpleasant tasks on somebody's shoulders just because he doesn't *complain*.

Or should that depend on the somebody?

Paul Perkins doesn't agree. He thinks the staff is going too far in passing off all their extra duties on Mr. Aidact. I want to support my teachers, but if this continues, Paul might report us to the Department of Education. That would be an unnecessary complication.

It's such an honor that Brightling was chosen out of thousands of middle schools to host this project. What a vote of confidence in me as principal that the Department of Education entrusted me with this responsibility. I wish I could tell everyone about it—but, of course, secrecy is part of the original agreement. The teachers know, naturally, but not the students or their parents. At the end of the year, this will all become public. Then the name Brightling Middle School will be in every newspaper, magazine, and podcast. It's hard to keep silent on such big news, but the rewards will be more than worth the wait.

I lean back in my swivel chair and gaze out into the hall at the 1974 state cup on its pedestal. Oh, sure, I know the kids think it's no big deal, but it represents field hockey supremacy—our school being the best at something. And 1974 was such a long time ago. Especially since we're not going to be winning that trophy again anytime soon. Maeve Delisle—who coached the team forever—retired last year. The girls should be in training already. The competition almost certainly is. If we can't find a new coach soon, Brightling will have to withdraw from the season.

I offered to coach the team myself, but our superintendent put the kibosh on that idea. She called it a "poor message for the community that our principals have extra time on their hands." It was disappointing—especially since I considered myself the Bobcats' last chance. For sure, today isn't the perfect time to recruit a field hockey coach. The commodore of a yacht club, maybe. The pitch is practically underwater. Any potential coach would picture themselves slogging through this weather, trying to run a practice in a swamp. Why, you'd need a candidate who doesn't have the sense to come in out of the rain. . . .

I whip back around to face the front window and the unloading of the last bus. There's my next field hockey coach, half-drowned and incapable of knowing it. Of course! Why didn't I think of it sooner? Kelly Tapper had the answer when she needed a colleague to cover detention during that plumbing emergency. *He doesn't complain.* Those were her exact words. He'll take over detention or lunchroom duty or cover recess. He'll even unload the buses during a certifiable hurricane. And when a girls' field hockey team needs a coach, he's your man.

Suddenly filled with energy, I leap to my feet, grab my umbrella, and head for the front entrance. As I pass the trophy in the hall, I reach out my elbow and polish away a fingerprint with my sleeve.

The instant I step outside, the wind tears the umbrella out of my hands, sending it tumbling across the lawn.

Soaked to the skin, I press on until I'm standing next to Mr. Aidact. I'm like a waterlogged rat, but he looks great, in spite of the droplets streaming down his face.

"Good morning, Principal Candiotti," he greets me, as if, for all the world, we'd just met over tea in the faculty lounge.

"Mr. Aidact," I bubble, "I have a question for you. What do you know about girls' field hockey?"

He tilts his head slightly in that way he has. Five or six seconds go by before he announces, "I know everything about it."

I beam at my newest staff member. "That's exactly what I wanted to hear."

Rosalie Arnette

When I see that they posted the roster for the Bobcats' girls' field hockey team, my heart jumps into my throat. And when I see my name partway down the list—

"I made it!" I breathe, punching the air.

Cassidy shoots me a quizzical look. "Everybody makes it. If you show up at tryouts, you're in."

Well, being a Bobcat might be no big deal for Cassidy, who's a multisport athlete and our captain besides. But for me, it's huge. This might be the proudest moment of my school career—except for the time I got 104 percent on the state math exam because I nailed both bonus questions. And maybe my first-place finish at the science fair last year. And that chess tournament—

Okay, so maybe this is only my fourth-proudest moment, but I'm celebrating it anyway. I'm terrible at tennis, I stink at softball, and at track I have two left feet. Soccer's a problem because I refuse to bounce the ball off my head. Sorry, not doing it. It looks goofy and it hurts. Field hockey is my only chance to have something on my record that says Rosalie Arnette is more than just brains and ambition. She's an athlete—and at a *good* sport too, not one of those other ones. I'm probably getting ahead of myself here, because I'm only in seventh grade, but this is going to look great on my college applications.

The field hockey coach is Mr. Aidact. That surprises me at first. Shouldn't a girls' team have a female coach? But just like he's supersmart at teaching, he's supersmart at field hockey too. At our very first team meeting, he stands up in front of the whiteboard and starts diagramming Xs, Ys, and Zs, with arrows all over the place. I swear, I've never been so confused in my life. So I look over at Cassidy, and she's just as lost as I am. That has to be brilliant coaching, confirmed.

We change into our teal-and-white "skorts"—kind of hideous, but what middle school has its uniforms supplied by a fashion designer? It's time to start training.

I've held an ice hockey stick a few times. This is totally different. It's shorter, which forces you into kind of a bent-over position that is even more bent-over when you're tall to begin with. And there's no real blade—it's rounded into a hooklike shape. Not only that, but only one side of the stick is flat. The other side is rounded, so you can't use it. It's not just hard—it's actually illegal. If you touch the ball with the rounded side of your stick, the whistle sounds, and your team loses possession.

"Don't worry about that too much," Cassidy confides to some of us seventh-grade newbies. "The field is so big that the refs miss a lot of those fouls."

Wrong. Mr. Aidact catches every single one of them. Even if the ball bounces off the round part of your stick by mistake, he sees it from sixty yards away. He must have eagle eyes or something. At practice, his whistle shrills constantly, like a cicada infestation. After the first few days, I'm hearing it in my sleep.

Coach Aidact also has us doing shooting drills. After all, you'll never win if you can't score goals. In theory, it should be easy. The nets are gigantic—twelve feet wide and seven feet high, with only one goalkeeper standing in the middle. But it's practically impossible because the sticks are so awkward. The first time I try it, I miss. Not the net; the ball. The second time, I fan over top of it, and the ball rolls about a yard and a half, coming to rest at the feet of Leticia Dooley, our goalie. Even the eighth graders struggle for power and accuracy.

So the coach decides to demonstrate for us. He practically has to fold himself in half to hold that super-short stick. "You use your body to aim," he explains. "Draw an imaginary line through your shoulders. That's the path your shot will take."

I'm surprised. "Did you play field hockey, Coach?"

"Never even once," he replies honestly. "Now, watch as I step into my shot with the opposite leg—"

He lunges forward, rears back his stick, and takes a mighty swing. There's a sharp *tock* and the ball takes off like it was fired out of a bazooka. By the time Leticia sees it, it's already behind her. It tears through the netting, bounces off the side of the field house, and soars into the parking lot. There's a crash followed by the wail of a car alarm.

Mr. Perkins, who's been seated in the bleachers, watching our practice and writing in his notebook, suddenly leaps to his feet. "My car!" High-stepping along the seats, he exits the stands at speed, his giant briefcase smacking against his knee. He runs into the lot, stopping at a white Toyota Prius. The windshield is a spiderweb of broken glass, with the ball lodged dead center, like a pimple.

It's a strange moment. Half the girls are horrified, while the others are holding in laughter. Weirder still, Coach Aidact goes on with his explanation of shooting technique like nothing just happened and his student teacher isn't melting down in the parking lot.

"Coach?" I venture shyly. "Shouldn't you go over there and—you know—help Mr. Perkins?"

He gives me that blue-eyed stare of his. "Do you have a field hockey question, Rosalie?"

"Uh—I guess not."

"Then let's save it till after practice," he concludes. "Now, everybody take a ball. . . ."

An all-too-familiar voice declares, "Snack time!"

Across the grass marches my mother, a medium-size carton balanced on her shoulder. I squint at the logo: FLAXPLOSION.

I rush over. "What are you doing here, Mom? We're in the middle of a practice!"

"Well, surely you can pause for a little quick energy," she reasons. She puts the box down, throws open the lid, and hollers, "Come and get it!"

The Bobcats, eager for a break, gather around. But

when they see the contents of the box, everyone backs off. Nobody reaches for a single one.

People tell me I look like my mother. But at this moment, I'm trying to look like anybody else.

Mom plucks a bar out of the carton, tears off the wrapper, and hands it to me. "All right, who's next?"

There are no takers.

"Is this your mom, Rosalie?" Leticia pipes up.

The girls are all looking at me like I've done something unforgivable.

I swear I'm tempted to say no. She means well, and she works hard for the PTA. But why, oh why, does the entire field hockey team—including the *eighth graders*—have to know that I'm the daughter of the person who chose these awful bars for the fundraiser? The school office is piled high with boxes just like this one. The students are supposed to be selling them to raise money for the Halloween dance. And anybody who's tried has had a lot of doors slammed in their faces, because they look terrible and taste worse!

"I *would* have one," Cassidy ventures carefully, "but if we eat too many ourselves, we won't have any left to sell."

"I might have been a *teeny* bit optimistic when I

placed the order," my mother admits. "Sales aren't as brisk as I was expecting."

"I took two dozen to sell," Ainsley whispers beside me. "I had to throw them in the garbage and pay the money out of my own pocket."

"It's worth it," I hear somebody else comment.

My face feels so hot I'm sure my cheeks are bright red.

Coach Aidact picks up a bar and examines the ingredients on the wrapper. "It seems healthy enough."

"*Thank* you!" Mom exclaims in an exaggerated tone. She holds out her hand. "Peggy Arnette, PTA president." She adds, "Well, Arnette is my *married* name. I'm recently divorced. The old habits die hard, don't you know."

Suddenly, I'm praying for the cleats on my shoes to turn into tiny drills to dig me down to the earth's core.

"Rob Aidact. Nice to meet you." They shake hands.

"Aidact," she repeats. "Is that German? Maybe Dutch?"

"A little of this and that," Mr. Aidact replies.

"Well, this is really interesting," I lie, "but we're wasting practice time."

"I'm sure you can break early just this once." Mom's eyes are on Mr. Aidact, not me.

Mr. Perkins slouches onto the scene, heels dragging,

the picture of dejection. "We're here for a while," he announces tragically. "The auto-glass repair people can't make it for another hour."

"Well, then"—Coach Aidact hefts his stick—"let's get back to work."

"Take a bar at least," Mom insists, pushing a Flax-plosion in his direction and not giving in until he accepts it. "It builds muscle tone." She looks him up and down. "Not that you have any problem in that department."

Oh, barf.

He slips it into the pocket of his sweatpants, but I notice that, for the rest of practice, he never takes a bite.

CONFIDENTIAL REPORT

To: Department of Education, Washington, DC
From: Paul Perkins, PE
Project: AIDACT

A concerning trend has begun to appear. Teachers are sloughing off unwanted duties on AIDACT. This results in AIDACT being involved in activities outside the parameters of the project, including even coaching a sport. There is increased risk of a security breach when AIDACT interacts with anything outside Department planning (see attached document: field hockey ball). A PTA member could present a future problem, but this is under control at the moment.

PROJECT STATUS: Green

SPECIAL EXPENSES
One windshield for Toyota Prius

Nathan Popova

Oliver punches in the code and I watch as his garage door slowly rises off the concrete floor.

"What do you think?" he asks proudly.

A Big Wheel sits in the middle of the garage—the girl kind, pink, lavender, and white, with multicolored streamers coming out of the handlebars and the back of the seat.

I frown at him. "What are we supposed to do with that?"

He beams. "We're going to change history at our school."

When you've been friends with Oliver as long as I have, you get used to the big talk. In kindergarten, when we poured the milk for snack time into the finger paint, he called it "cowification." Last year, he spent half of sixth grade wishing everybody a very loud *"Greetings!"* because *hi* wasn't good enough. He's kind of larger-than-life. So when I hear "change history," I don't take it too seriously. It's just Oliver being Oliver.

"Change history how?"

"We're rule-wreckers." He shrugs. "And it's time to take down the great-grandfather of all dumb rules."

That's when it comes to me. "Not the Big Wheel thing!"

He nods, and I can see the excitement in his eyes. "I'm going to do it! I'm going to ride this Big Wheel up and down the main hall, and the whole school is going to see me."

My Oliver Alert kicks in—not a full alarm yet, but a steady warning beep. "Seems to me we're already in detention because of the prank with the cars. How do you think you're going to get away with this one?"

"Easy. I'll do it when there's nobody else around. You'll shoot it with your phone and post it on the seventh-grade chat."

"Teachers can get on the seventh-grade chat too, you

know," I point out. "They'll see your face, and that'll be the end of you. You'll get expelled, and me too, because who else would let you talk them into shooting the video?"

"They won't recognize me," he declares triumphantly. "I'll be wearing a mask."

"Oh, sure," I snort. "Like a guy in a mask can just waltz past security into a school."

"That's not going to be a problem." His eyes light up the way they always do when he's figured something out. "Because we're going to do this on the one night that *everyone's* wearing a mask."

"When's that?" I challenge.

"Halloween. They'll be letting people into the school to go to the dance. But since everyone will be in the gym, the hallways will be empty. We can film to our hearts' content."

The Oliver Alert volume level swells to a deafening horn. It's so loud that all I can say is, "Wow."

"I know, right? Simple, yet brilliant too. Tell you what—I'll even give you a turn on the Big Wheel."

Oliver Alert! . . . Oliver Alert! . . . Abandon Ship! . . .

The weirdest part is I know I'm going to do it. I *hear* the Oliver Alerts, but for some reason, I never listen to them, even though I totally get that we're headed for disaster. There's just something irresistible about the guy. And sooner or later, I'll be in—just like I was in for the cars and Fire in the Hole and all those other pranks dating back to the milk-in-the-finger-paint stunt. When the milk went sour, our classroom stank, and nobody could figure out why. But I listened to Oliver and kept my mouth shut, even when the school called in an exterminator because they thought there might be a dead raccoon in the walls.

We were five years old, but nothing was different. Rules were made to be wrecked.

✳

The whole week leading up to the Halloween dance, the excitement growing inside Oliver threatens to lift his feet off the ground and carry him away. For him, the only thing better than the perfect prank is the anticipation. Even when we're sitting in detention, I'll look over and see him smiling. In his mind, he's already on that Big Wheel, tearing up and down the school.

Also, he's constantly whispering in my ear, fine-tuning the plan. It's hard to understand whispering during a full-blown Oliver Alert.

"Have you figured out what your other costume is going to be?" he hisses on Wednesday.

I check to make sure Mr. Aidact is on the far side of the room, out of earshot, before I reply. "*Other* costume? I thought we're both going as the Grim Reaper. Why do I need another costume?"

He's way ahead of me, as usual. "If we wear our Grim Reaper suits on the Big Wheel, everybody's going to know it's us. We need two costumes—one for the dance and one for the video."

"I'm not changing clothes in the middle of the school," I protest. "The only thing worse than getting expelled is getting expelled in your underwear."

He shakes his head. "The Reaper robes go *over* the other outfit. So when we're ready to film, we throw off costume number one and we're already in costume number two. I'd go with something tight for the inner layer. I've got a Batman suit from fifth grade that might still fit. We'll check out your closet after school."

I clam up because Mr. Aidact is coming our way.

Stinky Newhouse throws out a line: "*What's poppin'?*"

"*Brand-new whip, just hopped in,*" Mr. Aidact spits back.

They smile at each other and bump fists.

Detention sure is different now that the new teacher is running things. It used to have a solemn atmosphere, where the lawbreakers of the school went to be punished for their crimes. Now it's turned into a game of Stump Mr. Aidact, who seems to have memorized every song lyric in history. It started with Stinky and rap songs, but now kids grill him with lines from pop, rock, country, heavy metal, reggae, punk, show tunes, and alternative. Mr. Aidact always has the answer. Even Oliver got in on the action. Last night, he spent an hour memorizing part of an opera that's all in German. Without even missing a beat, Mr. Aidact rattled off what comes next. (At least I'm guessing that's what it was. I don't speak German.)

Mr. Perkins is pretty salty about the whole thing. I don't think he loves it when Mr. Aidact has jobs beyond being his supervising teacher. He doesn't like it that Mr. Aidact is coaching girls' field hockey either. What he really hates is when there's a conflict between the two, and he has to cover detention.

"That's not my job," I overhear him complaining to Principal Candiotti.

Seems to me student teachers learn to be real teachers by doing teacher things. If that's not his job, what is? That guy is way too cranky to be a teacher. He needs a career more suited to his personality, like professional hermit or the person in every neighborhood who tells kids to get off his lawn.

The day of the Halloween dance isn't much of a school day because most classes are working on last-minute decorations for the gym. The teachers aren't thrilled about it, but the PTA ran out of money, so we have to improvise. Nobody sold the gross flax bars that were supposed to be our big fundraiser, which means everything we can't afford to buy, we have to make ourselves. It isn't going to look very slick, but the deejay wouldn't cut his price, so the entire budget is going to him.

Even detention gets in on the act. We spend the hour cutting out stencils of pumpkins, witches, and black cats, and making a black-and-orange paper chain.

"Why are we doing this?" Stinky complains, as five of eight legs drop off his stenciled spider. "What is this for?"

"For the *dance*," supplies Mia, who spends almost as much time in detention as Stinky, due to chronic lateness.

"What dance?" Stinky demands.

"The Halloween dance," Oliver tells him.

Stinky is mystified. "When's that?"

"Tonight!" Mia explodes.

"That's why we don't call it the Groundhog Day

Dance," Oliver adds. "Because it isn't Groundhog Day. It's Halloween."

"Well, I'm not going to any dance," Stinky grumbles.

"Why not?" puts in Mr. Aidact.

"It's stupid."

"A dance is a social gathering," Mr. Aidact lectures. "It can be neither smart nor stupid."

"There's going to be a deejay," Mia adds. "You like music."

"I don't have a costume," Stinky mutters.

"Just draw a fake mustache with Magic Marker," Oliver tells him. "You don't want to miss this. The place is going to be on wheels!"

I almost break my neck whipping my head around to glare at him, my Oliver Alert blaring. We're doing something so against the rules that our next stretch in detention could be a hundred years, and he's dropping hints in front of a teacher!

Oliver winks at me.

I don't wink back.

11

Oliver Zahn

I guess I grew a lot more than I thought since fifth grade. When I take out the Batman costume, it looks like an outfit for one of those American Girl dolls. Well, not that small, but you get the picture.

I'm stuck with it, though. The Halloween dance starts in less than an hour. It's too late to come up with a plan B. So I strip down to my skivvies, step into the "feet," and pull the stretchy polyester fabric all the way up. It's a pretty tight squeeze—especially if you want to breathe—and I practically have to dislocate both shoulders to get the arms in. I read somewhere that Houdini had to do that to escape from a straitjacket. Well, if he could do it in the name of stardom, I can do it in the name of rule-wrecking.

I throw on the cape and the headpiece and examine myself in the mirror. Wow, I look like I've been spray-painted gray. It's so tight that you can tell that my belly button is an "innie," not an "outie." It's pretty humiliating. The good news is that I've got the Grim Reaper cloak to cover it up with and a skeleton mask to complete the outfit. I'm only going to be Batman when I'm riding the Big Wheel on the video—and no one's going to know that's me.

"Leaving now," I call to my parents. "I won't be too late."

My mom catches up with me in the hall. "You be careful, Oliver. There are high schoolers out there, picking on the younger ones and stealing their candy."

"I'm not going trick-or-treating," I tell her. "I'm just going to the dance."

There are a lot of little kids on the street already, and I make a big show of pretending to be scared by their costumes, even the girl dressed as a Crayola crayon. I think they're a lot more scared by me. The skeleton mask is really creepy. The kids are all carrying loot bags. Me too. Mine isn't for candy, though. I'm hoping nobody notices that mine is shaped exactly like a Big Wheel. My Batman headpiece is in there too.

I arrive at Nathan's house at the same time as a group of trick-or-treaters, and Nathan's dad tosses a couple of Tootsie Pops into my bag. They make a loud rattling sound as they bounce off the Big Wheel.

"That's quite a stash you've got there, kid," he comments. "How long have you been out here—since last week?"

"It's me, Mr. Popova. Oliver."

When Nathan comes down the stairs, I realize that I got off easy with the Batman suit. His family threw out all his old costumes, so he had to improvise what to put on under the Grim Reaper robes. He's wearing his mom's pink Lululemon leggings and a black T-shirt that reads DEATH BEFORE DISHONOR. I can see his eyes burning at me through the eyeholes of his skeleton mask.

"It's not that bad," I assure him.

"It's worse," he says mournfully. "These Lululemons look like I forgot to put on any pants."

"When the robe's closed, all that will be covered," I soothe. "Where's your Big Wheel mask?"

He slips a second mask into the bag and we set out

for school. He carries both scythes, since I've got the bulky sack.

The closer we get to Brightling, the more we're on the alert. A lot of kids are arriving for the dance, clustering on the lawn, pointing and laughing, admiring one another's costumes. Keeping to the shadows, we avoid the crowd and stash the big bag in the cover of some bushes close to the side entrance. Then we put on our skeleton masks and join the group out front to make sure everyone sees us—two Grim Reapers, and not Batman and the Lululemon guy at all.

There are a few other Reapers, and the usual assortment of ghosts, wizards, and witches. The football players, as usual, are too lazy to put on costumes and just wear their uniforms. Rosalie is dressed up as Marie Curie, with glowing stones taped all over her white lab coat. Laki is a medieval knight, waving his six-foot-long plastic lance far too close to people's faces. Ainsley is a chipmunk. A group of six eighth graders is the hit of the night so far. They've stitched themselves together into a multicolored caterpillar. They're having a little trouble walking, but they're an amazing sight. I'm really impressed—but, obviously, I've got bigger things to worry about in the coming hours.

At exactly six thirty, they open the doors to the gym and we all pour inside. The place looks pretty good for an amateur decorating job. Most of the credit for that goes to the deejay's special effects—bubbles rising, clouds of mist, and multicolored laser lights cutting the air. A lot of teachers are there as chaperones, including Principal Candiotti. I spot Mr. Aidact, who is methodically blowing up orange and black balloons using a helium tank. Rosalie's mom is with him, talking a blue streak.

Nathan sidles up to me. "Check out Perkins. He brought that giant briefcase. I wonder what he keeps in there?"

"Probably his personality," I reply. "He doesn't want it to escape."

Nathan doesn't answer. He's staring at the door, where Stinky has just entered the gym. The detention king isn't wearing a costume or even a mask. Also, he didn't take my advice and draw on a fake mustache. There are only two things different about him. First, the word *ME* is written across his forehead in bright green Magic Marker. Second, clutched in his left hand is a sleek, silvery fish.

Nathan and I practically break our legs getting over to him.

"Stinky!" I exclaim. "Glad you're here! Love the costume—great idea to come as . . ." I pause, hoping he'll finish the sentence for me.

"That shows what you know," Stinky shoots back. "I'm not wearing a costume. I'm—" And he points to his forehead.

"Awesome," Nathan puts in. "You're yourself. And . . . ?" He gestures toward the scaly form in the eighth grader's fist.

"Everybody thinks my name is Stinky—which it's *not*!" he tells us with his usual aggrieved expression. "So when I started thinking about what I wanted to go as, I didn't want to be a fireman or secretary of the navy or anything dumb like that. I just want to be me, so I wrote it right on my forehead."

"And why the fish?" I inquire.

"I don't stink. So I brought along something that *does* to show people the difference. *Me*"—he points to his forehead—"*Stinky*." He brandishes the fish and then holds it up to his nose. "At least it *will* stink. It's still a little frozen. Stupid fish."

At that moment, the sound system blasts to life with the first song of the night.

"Gotta fly," Stinky tells us briskly. "I need to request some music that doesn't come from a kindergartner's birthday party playlist." He hustles off to the deejay station, fish held high.

"I feel like we should be doing something, but I have no idea what," Nathan muses nervously.

I shrug. "What are we supposed to do? He's an eighth grader. He could probably kill us."

"But we're letting him make an idiot out of himself!"

"No, we're not," I insist. "The place is packed; the air is full of mist and bubbles; there are costumes everywhere you look. Who's going to notice one little fish—at least till it starts to defrost? Relax. We've got a rule to take down tonight."

Nathan stiffens his jaw, which makes the bony "chin" of his skeleton mask jut out. Poor kid. He doesn't have the stomach for this kind of operation.

I have to hand it to Rosalie's mom. She may have laid an egg with those poison flax bars for the fundraiser that didn't raise any funds, but she sure hired a great deejay, no matter what Stinky says. Pretty soon, the gym is jumping and the noise is off the charts. The dance floor is packed with gyrating costumes and the snack and drink tables are mobbed. It's the perfect kind of party for sneaking out of, since the teachers are completely overwhelmed by the sights and sounds. No one is misbehaving yet, but it's so wild that it looks like

Halloween could dissolve into chaos in the blink of an eye. Out of all the faculty, only Mr. Aidact seems calm and detached, because Mr. Aidact is always calm and detached. I have to admit he's a very chill guy.

When his back is turned, we slip from the gym and dash to the side entrance. Nathan holds the door open and I haul the bag with the Big Wheel out of the bushes and inside. We wrestle the pink-and-lavender kiddie bike out into the open, rip off our Grim Reaper robes, and switch masks. I replace mine with the Batman head-piece. I have to snicker at Nathan's—he's Squidward, complete with a bouncy rubber nose.

We don't have to worry about being quiet. The noise coming out of the gym is so loud that they couldn't hear us if we were screaming and banging drums. The entire school building pulses with the heavy beat from the dee-jay's sound system and the pounding feet on the dance floor.

Nathan gulps. "All right, where do we do this?"

"Right outside the office," I reply. "Where all dumb rules come from." I feel my chest swelling with pride—or maybe that's just the skintight Batman suit. I'm experiencing the satisfaction of seeing a plan come together perfectly. A couple of minutes ago, we were two Grim Reapers at a school dance. Now we're Batman and

Lulu-Squidward—and the school hall is 100 percent empty and 100 percent ours.

We set up just outside the office doors with Nathan filming on his phone. I bend myself into a painful pretzel climbing onto the undersize Big Wheel. Nathan has to place my feet on the pink pedals. At this point, my knees are practically behind my ears. I know a moment of uncertainty. Am I actually going to be able to make this thing go? Will it still count as rule-wrecking if Nathan has to push me down the hall? After all, the rule says you can't *ride* a Big Wheel in school. There's nothing in the student handbook against sitting paralyzed on one, pushing against the pedals, grunting.

And then my legs start to move, sending the Big Wheel rolling slowly down the corridor. "Start shooting!" I holler at my cameraman as I pick up speed.

And pretty soon I'm doing it—lumbering along on noisy plastic wheels, cruising past trophy cases, bulletin boards, and pictures of graduating classes from decades long ago. My right hip is killing me, but at least I know I won't limp, because my left knee hurts even worse. And anyway, it's all worth it for a rule well wrecked.

Now comes the hard part—the U-turn at the end of the hall. Luckily, the entrance to the library is wide. Otherwise, I would have hit the wall and been stuck there forever. I stall out a couple of times, but I manage to get myself headed in the right direction. I come roaring up the corridor at my cameraman, grinning in triumph—which is a waste of effort, since no one will be able to see my face behind the Batman mask. By the time I reach Nathan, he has to jump out of the way because I'm free-wheeling. The dismount isn't very graceful. Okay, I fall off and my nose bleeds a little.

"Did you get it?" I pant. "Tell me you got it!"

"I got it!" he crows.

Hunched over his screen, we watch the video right then and there. It's a thing of beauty. It looks like what it is—a ridiculous rule exposed for all to see. It looks like justice.

On the spot, we upload it to the seventh-grade chat. We use the name Freedom Avenger and title the clip *Section 24-B*. That's the part of the *Code of Student Behavior* where the no–Big Wheels rule is written down.

Nathan exhales in relief. "It's over! Let's get back to the dance!"

"But you haven't had a turn yet!"

"I don't want a turn," he counters. "I just want to get back in my Reaper costume and survive this night."

I'm adamant. "You'll never forgive yourself if you don't take a ride. It's epic!"

"I believe you. Now let's get out of here—"

"No!" I grab him by the shoulders and force him onto the Big Wheel. Either he's a lot more flexible than I am, or those Lululemons really are amazing workout pants, because his legs allow his feet to go right on the pedals, no problem.

He isn't moving, though, so I reach out with my foot and give the Big Wheel a mighty shove. And that is a major mistake.

Nathan takes off at a sharp angle, ricocheting off the wall.

"Steer!" I shout.

And he does—straight into the pedestal that holds the 1974 girls' state championship field hockey trophy. The impact launches him free of the Big Wheel. At the last second, he holds up his hands to protect his face, and his flailing elbow knocks the trophy off the pedestal.

The shiny award, pride of Brightling, sails through the air and smashes into pieces as it bounces along the tile floor. The wooden base breaks off; the winged victory figure is de-winged and decapitated; one handle snaps away; and the cup itself is battered and dented beyond recognition.

Through the Squidward head, I can see the horror in Nathan's eyes. "We're *dead*! We're so dead! Mrs.

81

Candiotti loves this trophy more than she loves *Mr.* Candiotti! Look what you made me do!"

"Maybe it's not so bad. We can collect the pieces, glue them together—"

"Oh, sure! And no one's going to notice that the cup part looks like somebody ran over it with a cement mixer!" he rages.

He's right. "We've got to hide the evidence!" I whip my Batman cape over my head and spread it out on the floor. We gather up what's left of the trophy and tie the cape into a bundle.

"What about the Big Wheel?" Nathan wheezes.

"Leave it," I decide. "I found it in the garbage. There's no way anybody can tie it to us."

We retrace our steps to the side entrance, where we left our stuff. We switch back to the skeleton masks and shrug into our Grim Reaper robes.

I open up the custodian's closet and pull out two shovels.

Nathan is distraught. "What are those for?"

"We're going to bury the broken you-know-what in the sandpit. It'll be like it never existed."

"Tell that to Mrs. Candiotti," he shoots back. "She passes that pedestal twenty times a day. And what's she going to see? Nothing!"

"It's better than finding it all smashed to pieces," I reason. "Now grab a shovel and let's go."

Stepping out of the building into the chilly Halloween night takes away what's left of our breath. The pounding music from the dance is even louder out here, since the high gym windows are open. We can see as far as the street, where little kids in colorful costumes swarm everywhere. I hope nobody notices two Grim Reapers, carrying shovels instead of scythes, heading for the athletic field to bury incriminating evidence.

"I can't believe what we're doing right now," Nathan moans.

I try to put a positive spin on it. "This happens in rule-wrecking every now and then. You have to be able to think on your feet and improvise." To be honest, I'm pretty freaked-out myself. It shows how wrong things can go. You start out riding a Big Wheel and before you know it, you're burying a beloved trophy behind the school.

The blacktop is lighted, but once we reach the running track, we have to use our phones to see in the inky darkness. The sandpit is in the middle, where the jumping events are held, but we have trouble finding it until Nathan stubs his toe and falls face-first into it. He comes up, spitting sand.

We start to dig. What a mess! It rained last night, so under the surface layer of dry sand is pure mud. If we weren't so frantic, we wouldn't be pelting each other with dirt. But it's dark, so we can't see where our shovels are throwing. Plus we're in a hurry to get this over with quick so we can sneak back into the dance to pretend we were never gone.

"Do you think it's deep enough yet?" Nathan pants.

I shine my phone light into the hole. "It'll have to do." I drop my shovel and pick up the cape-bundle containing the broken trophy pieces—and a large hand grabs my wrist.

"Now, what have we here?" asks a deep, snarky voice from behind me.

Several phones shine on Nathan and me, lighting us up in the sandpit. Five hulking high school guys surround us, close and menacing.

"N-nothing!" I stammer. "We're just—digging."

"Dude, they're burying their candy!" exclaims the biggest of the five. "How stupid can you get? The ants'll eat it!"

"Correction"—the first kid shakes his head—"*I'm* going to eat it." He rips the bundle from my hands.

"But it isn't candy—" Nathan begins.

Laughing and trading high fives, they shove us into

the pit and kick sand and mud all over us. With a chorus of "So long, suckers!" and "Eat dirt!" and "Happy Halloween!" they run off into the night, waving the bundle of trophy pieces triumphantly over their heads.

We crawl back onto the grass, spitting sand and grime.

"*Now* what are we going to do?" Nathan laments.

"Nothing," I decide. "We came out here to disappear that trophy, and it's gone."

We pick ourselves up off the ground, grab the shovels, and begin to trudge back to the school.

"I'm never going to forgive you for this, man," Nathan says bitterly. "This is the worst night of my life!"

"I'll bet I can make you smile," I retort.

"I may never smile again!" he seethes.

"Just picture those high school jerks opening up the cape expecting to find it full of candy."

By the time we make it back to the school, we're both snickering.

We head straight to the gym, slip inside, and immediately melt into the crowd. To our enormous relief, nobody seems to have noticed we were missing. How could they? The Halloween dance is shaping up into one of the greatest middle school bashes of all time. The sound system is cranked up so loud that the basketball nets are vibrating with the pounding bass. So many kids are dancing that the floor is actually moving under our feet. Stinky gyrates atop one of the giant speaker towers, punching the air with his half-crushed fish in time with the beat. Sweat runs down from his hairline, washing the *ME* on his forehead into his bushy unibrow.

Nathan elbows me in the ribs, his horror evident through the eyeholes of his mask.

"What's the problem?" I ask. "Nobody saw us come in."

"The shovels!" he hisses. "We've still got the shovels!"

I stare at the muddy implement in my hands. Oh man, talk about an amateur mistake. In all the excitement of getting jumped by those high school kids, we forgot to put back the shovels and pick up our scythes.

"We can fix it!" I begin. "We'll go back to the custodian's closet—"

At that moment the music dies abruptly, and the deejay shines a spotlight on Mrs. Arnette. "All right, people! We'll get back to the music and the fun, but right now, I want everybody to line up for the Best Costume contest!"

Nathan gestures desperately in the direction of the exit. I shake my head. It's too late to slip out unnoticed now. All we can do is join the slow parade past the judges and hope nobody notices that two Grim Reapers are carrying shovels instead of scythes.

As we make our way into the long queue, the deejay brings up the lights in the gym, and that's when I get my first good look at myself and Nathan. Our robes are covered in sand and dirt, and every step rains grime. Heart sinking, I try to walk in Nathan's footsteps to avoid leaving a second set of muddy prints on the parquet floor.

As we shuffle along the line, Coach Gilderoy scorches me with a furious glare. His specialty is basketball, and the polished gym floor is his pride and joy. I sense that the first chance he gets, he's going to sentence us to ten thousand push-ups in PE.

The three judges are Mrs. Arnette, Mrs. Berg, and Mr. Aidact. Since basically every kid in school is in costume, it takes twenty minutes for us all to make our way past the judging table. When we finally get there, Nathan tries to hide his shovel in the folds of his robes. I take the opposite approach, holding it over my head in triumph. If I have to be stuck with a shovel, I'm going to act like I'm supposed to have it. Never let the teachers see you look guilty—especially when you're guilty as sin. The lady judges make notes, but not Mr. Aidact, who just peers at us with those intense eyes.

At last, the viewing is over, and the music comes back on while the three judges confer. I grab Nathan and drag him out onto the dance floor. Not that I have any interest in dancing, but it's a good way to escape Mr. Aidact's steady blue gaze. We sidle over to Rosalie. She's dancing with Kevin, who's wearing a bushy white wig— Marie Curie and Albert Einstein. Classic Kevin, always pretending to be the genius he's not.

"Great party, Rosalie!" I call. "Your mom really pulled it off!"

Instead of saying thank you, she frowns with suspicion. "What's up with the shovels?"

"Yeah," Kevin chimes in. "What are the shovels for?"

Some of the dust from my robes finds its way up Kevin's nose, and he lets out a mighty sneeze. His big wig topples off his head and Nathan catches it neatly with his shovel.

"*That's* what the shovels are for," I supply, deadpan.

"But didn't you guys have scythes when you got here?" Rosalie persists. "Grim Reapers carry scythes."

The general buzz of conversation covers our silence as kids speculate on their favorites to win the contest.

One voice asks, "Hey, does anybody else smell fish?"

I sniff. He's right. I guess Stinky's un-costume has

finally started to defrost—although the fishy odor isn't very noticeable amid the sweat and Axe body spray.

Just then the music cuts out and Mrs. Arnette grabs the microphone again. "The judges have come to their decision! The winners of the best costume contest are— *the two gravediggers!*"

There's a smattering of applause, but mostly, a confused murmur ripples through the gym. Gravediggers? What gravediggers? I admit I haven't been here for a lot of the dance, but I've had a pretty good look around. I definitely don't see any gravediggers.

"The attention to detail in these costumes is impressive," Mrs. Arnette goes on. "The dirt on their shovels and even on their robes—you really believe they've been digging—"

That's when the deejay's spotlight shines on Nathan and me.

"Come on up, gravediggers, and take a well-deserved bow!"

Luckily, our ovation covers the sound of Kevin's big mouth: "But I thought they're supposed to be Grim Reapers!"

Because nobody sold any Flaxplosion bars, there wasn't enough money to buy a prize for the contest winners. So guess what we win—the unsold Flaxplosion bars. One carton each. Contents: 144 units.

Sometimes with these school contests, it's hard to tell the winners from the losers.

But the real prize will come later, when eight hundred kids head home from the dance and log into the seventh-grade chat. There they'll find our video of Rule 24-B, totally wrecked.

Nathan Popova

November starts off in the auditorium for an emergency assembly.

"I wonder what this is about," Kevin comments as Mr. Aidact and Mr. Perkins lead us to our seats. "Whatever they have to say—why didn't they tell us when we were all together at the dance last night?"

"Didn't you see the seventh-grade chat?" Ainsley challenges. "That Batman on the Big Wheel?"

Seems to me Oliver would have the brains to keep his mouth shut after all the yammering he's done about Rule 24-B. Think again.

"Yeah, but who was Batman?" he muses. "There was no Batman at the Halloween dance."

The Oliver Alert is pulsing through my entire body. It makes my stomach hurt—or maybe that's the Flaxplosion bar my mother made me have for breakfast. Only 143 to go.

"It can't be the Big Wheel thing," Rosalie argues. "Surely nobody cares about that old rule—not enough to drag eight hundred kids out of class the morning after the biggest party of the year."

"Quiet, everyone." Mr. Aidact settles us down. "Here comes Principal Candiotti."

The principal stalks to center stage with a look on her face like a judge about to sentence a convicted ax murderer. "Last night," she begins, her voice under tight control, "a terrible crime was committed against the entire Brightling community."

A perplexed murmur buzzes through the student body.

"I get that Big Wheels are against the rules," Kevin whispers. "But since when is it a 'terrible crime'?"

"While most of us were in the gym, dancing and having fun," the principal goes on, "somebody stole the state championship field hockey trophy from its pedestal in front of the office!"

Oliver and I don't dare look at each other. So that's what this is really all about—not the Big Wheel, the trophy. *Her* trophy! We should have known!

The principal rakes her students with eyes of flame. "A trophy is more than wood and brass. It represents greatness—not just from long ago, but the greatness we can all achieve if we apply ourselves and work together. It's the very best of Brightling Middle School, yesterday, today, and all the tomorrows still to come!"

My cheeks feel so hot that you could fry an egg on me. Every word out of Mrs. Candiotti's mouth is another knife-thrust between my ribs. I risk a quick glance at Oliver. My partner in crime radiates newborn-baby innocence. How does he do that?

"There can never be an excuse for this unforgivable act," the principal continues. "But because this trophy means so much to all of us, if it is returned to its pedestal, there will be no questions asked."

That might be the worst part of all—because I know something Mrs. Candiotti doesn't: there *is* no trophy; there are only pieces of trophy. And who knows where those pieces are? When the teenagers who stole them opened up the Batman cape and didn't find candy, they probably just tossed everything in a garbage can somewhere or dropped it down a sewer. This is an *ex*-trophy!

After the assembly, we're on our way back to home-room, marching behind Mr. Perkins's giant briefcase, when we pass the lost-and-found box in front of the cafeteria. Sitting on top of the usual assortment of sneakers, gym clothes, raincoats, and binders is the purple-and-pink Big Wheel.

"Now, that's annoying," Oliver murmurs beside me. "We go to all that trouble to wreck a rule, and they leave the Big Wheel just sitting here, like it isn't even illegal."

Oliver Alert! . . . Oliver Alert! . . .

"Shhh!" I hiss, grabbing his arm and pulling him along. "It's probably a trap. Whoever claims the Big Wheel took the trophy."

He nods. "Good thinking. That would explain why Candiotti never mentioned it during the assembly."

"She didn't have to. We posted it on the chat, remember? Seems to me half the school has seen it by now."

Oliver is still dissatisfied. "You'd think a principal would read her own *Code of Student Behavior.*"

By the time we make it to homeroom, the bell has already rung. As everybody grabs their book bags and heads off to first period, Mr. Aidact pulls us aside.

"Oliver, Nathan. I'd like a word with you two pupils."

"What's up, Mr. Aidact?" Oliver says casually.

I can't help noticing that Perkins has started writing in his notebook again.

Mr. Aidact holds his phone in front of us. "I'm sure you're familiar with the seventh-grade chat."

The video that plays on the screen is one we know all too well—Batman on the Big Wheel, pedaling madly up and down the main hall of Brightling.

Oliver has the nerve to exclaim, "Hey, isn't that against the rules?"

With his free hand, Mr. Aidact takes out a clear plastic ziplock snack bag. At first glance, it's empty. Then I notice a tiny gray thread trapped inside. "When you came up to accept your award last night, I picked this off your robe," he says to Oliver. "It's a perfect match for the color of a Batman suit."

Oliver's eyes widen in surprise, but he tries to brazen it out. "Well, maybe it's *similar*. . . ."

"It's a match of more than ninety-eight percent certainty. Which means that *you* are the Batman in the video. And since you two were costume partners, we can conclude that *you*"—now the blue eyes are on me—"were the cameraman for this video."

I don't say anything. I can't. My mouth is so dry it won't open. The Oliver Alert is an uninterrupted screech in my ears. Even Oliver, for once, is struck dumb. We wait for the new teacher to connect the dots—the Big Wheel . . . the main hall . . . the missing trophy.

"Was this another one of your pranks?" Mr. Aidact asks.

He doesn't see it! I practically have to swallow the words to keep from blurting them out loud. How can a guy who identified a Batman suit from a single thread overlook something so obvious? Why would he fail to notice a link between two things that happened in exactly the same place on exactly the same night?

I toss a sideways glance in the direction of Perkins, but the student teacher is still buried in his note making.

"We're sorry," Oliver says all too readily.

The blue-eyed gaze intensifies. "Legit?" Mr. Aidact probes.

Legit is not a word you expect to hear from a teacher who normally talks like somebody's butler. Where would he get it? For sure not from Perkins, the most boring man alive.

"Uh—yeah," I manage. "Legit."

"Two more weeks of detentions," Mr. Aidact pronounces.

Oliver heaves a heavy sigh of resignation, but it's an act.

We both know we got off easy.

Rosalie Arnette

Sometimes I wonder if I plan for the future too much and forget that I'm living in the present.

Like the whole field hockey thing. Oh, I know it'll look great on my school transcript. But now I'm starting to question whether that's even worth it anymore.

I thought it would be better, because Brightling has such a long field hockey tradition. After all, how many schools put a trophy for an all-girls sport on its own pedestal outside the office? And when the cup got stolen during the Halloween dance, that made it even cooler. Like a mystery—the Case of the Missing Championship.

Well, forget it. The trophy isn't a mystery; it's just gone. And everybody's already sick of talking about it, except Principal Candiotti, who's offered a hundred-dollar reward for its safe return. Even the other girls have lost interest—if they ever had much interest in field hockey to begin with. Nobody's really good besides Cassidy and maybe Leticia, who's rock-solid as our goalie. Most of the other eighth graders only care about how they look in their skorts and uniforms. They spend half their time posing for their boyfriends and other guys who hang around our practices.

The thing is, the older girls are supposed to be the *leaders*. And without them showing us what to do, we newbies can't really get into the flow of the play. I've been practicing for three weeks and I still have no idea what a real field hockey game is like. Oh, sure, I've trained every *skill*. But how do you put them all together, to become a real player? Beats me.

I hate to say it, but most of the blame should probably go to Mr. Aidact. He's never played field hockey—or any kind of hockey. He'll go on and on about rules and fundamentals and strategies, like "marking your man"—go figure: even in a girls' sport, the player you have to cover is your "man." He can lay on the details to the point where your head is spinning. And it's not that you don't understand him—you do. It's just that it's all theory—like how an electron orbits the nucleus of an atom in science. You believe that it's happening, but you can't *see* it.

I finally get my position. I'm a right back, which means I play defense on the right side. And that's pretty much all I know about it. I've gotten straight As every year since kindergarten; I'm captain of the mathletes and the seventh-grade quiz bowl team; when sixth graders need a tutor, Mrs. Rostenkowski sends them straight to me. But the first time an opposing player comes down the field at me, I'm going to have absolutely no idea what to do.

✳

We open our season on the road against the Sheridan Middle School Seahawks, about a twenty-minute ride away. I can't believe how the other girls are laughing and goofing around, while I'm paralyzed with nervousness. Don't they realize that we're about to make fools of ourselves in front of hundreds of people? We're a disgrace to our school, and I'm the only one who sees it!

Not far from Sheridan, we stop at a red light. And when it turns green, the bus shudders and dies. The driver twists the key again and again. Nothing.

For me, it's the last straw. The 1974 Bobcats made it all the way to the state championship, and we can't even get across town. But the other girls think this is an amazing adventure—like we're shipwrecked on a desert island or something. They're taking selfies and blowing up social media, while I want to disintegrate.

The driver and Coach Aidact are peering under the hood, trying to figure out what to do, when Mr. Perkins lugs that big briefcase of his off the bus and opens it up in the middle of the road. I run to the front window for a look at what he keeps in that thing. I figured it would have a lot of books and papers because he's a student teacher. No—it's full of tools! He selects a wrench, reaches into the engine, and makes some kind of adjustment. The next thing you know, *vroom!*—the bus starts up. And five minutes later, we're pulling into the circular driveway at Sheridan Middle School.

Remember my fear about making fools of ourselves in front of hundreds of people? Well, problem solved. The stands are empty except for a few parents and maybe a dozen kids, all from Sheridan. The only Bobcats fan is my mother—and I don't even think she came to see me. She wants to hang around Mr. Aidact.

She settles herself on the bleachers directly behind our bench. "Hi, sweetie!" she calls to me.

At least, I hope it's me she's calling to.

The Sheridan Seahawks are already warming up on the other side of the field. I can tell by the way their passes click and their shots sizzle that they're going to murder us. When they run with the ball, it's like it's glued to their sticks. All this time I've been learning field hockey without any picture of what it's supposed to look like. Now I know. It looks like what the Seahawks do and we don't.

I'm not picked for the starting eleven, so my season begins on the bench with the other subs. About three seconds in, the Sheridan captain—who would make a great linebacker for their football team—steals the ball and thunders down the field. Her teammates swarm around her, and the ball flashes between them like a laser beam reflected by a system of mirrors. Our defenders are standing around, flat-footed. They just can't keep up with what's happening. They've never seen anything like what's coming at them. Before you know it, we're down 1–0. Exactly half a minute has ticked off the clock.

Mr. Aidact doesn't blow his stack or throw down his clipboard in disgust or do any of the things that normal coaches do. He doesn't even have a clipboard. He stands stock-still and perfectly straight, watching every move on the field through those piercing blue eyes.

On the next possession, Cassidy tries to make a run for the Bobcats. She doesn't get halfway to the Seahawks' sixteen-yard circle. One of their midfielders effortlessly snatches the ball away from her and flips it high in the air toward her teammates downfield. Our attackers and midfielders just stare up at it like they're watching a passing plane. And by the time it comes back down, the Seahawks are on the attack again: 2–0.

I check the clock on the scoreboard and see that 33:18 still remains out of the thirty-five-minute first half.

Coach Aidact sends in the subs in an attempt to change our luck on the field. That's when I log my first minutes. And just as I suspected, being in a real game is nothing like practice.

First of all, the field is so big that, 90 percent of the time, the play is nowhere near you. So I bounce lightly on the balls of my feet, but honestly, I don't think it would make any difference if I did nothing at all.

It would be easier to concentrate if Mom wasn't cheering encouragement from the sidelines. *"Attaway, Rosie! Keep up the good work! You're doing great!"*

Seriously, how can she tell?

I keep my eyes on Ainsley, who's playing center back beside me. When she moves up, I do too. When she retreats, so do I. So far, so good.

It's kind of boring, though, and after a while, I lose focus. Big mistake. When the play comes my way, it's with the force of a herd of elephants that smell fresh-baked peanut butter cookies.

As usual, Captain Linebacker spearheads the attack. I'm as tall as her, but slower. By the time I move up to shut her down, she's already past me. Leticia makes the first save but gives a fat rebound. When I try to reach around my opponent to clear it, she backs into me and I get knocked flat. Then she trips over me, landing on my stomach and knocking the wind out of me.

The whistle blows. It's a penalty—on *me*.

"For what?" I bawl. "Getting crushed to death?"

The Seahawks' captain is awarded a penalty corner, which is a free pass from the spot where the circle meets the end line. She finds a teammate, who launches a guided missile straight into the back of the net: 3–0.

"Way to go, Rosalie," Cassidy mutters on the bench.

I chew on my mouth guard and don't reply. The last thing I need is to get on the bad side of eighth graders like Cassidy. They already blame me for every bone-headed move by the PTA. Thanks, Mom.

Coach Aidact comes to my defense. "Inside the sixteen-yard circle, it's established strategy: you trip over defenders in order to draw a penalty."

"Yeah, but Rosalie fell for it," Cassidy puts in bitterly.

"It was the other girl who fell," he corrects her. "On Rosalie."

We stare at him. Is that supposed to be coaching humor?

The butt kicking doesn't stop there. The Seahawks pull out their starters and sub in the backups. They clobber us too. By halftime, we're down 5–zip. We don't have a single shot on their goalie. I can count the number of times we've touched the ball on the fingers of one hand.

"Way to go, Bobcats!" Mom calls from the stands.

What game has she been watching?

We cluster around Mr. Aidact, panting into our Gatorade cups and waiting for his pep talk. Surely a coach has a lot to say after watching his team get completely and utterly demolished.

And he says . . . nothing. Not a word. We're gathered there, doubled over, sucking air, gulping drinks. The atmosphere is so thick with expectation you can almost squeeze it in your fist. And what does our coach have to offer us? No advice. No encouragement. Not even sympathy.

And the craziest part is I actually feel bad for Mr. Aidact. He's such a train wreck of a coach that I find myself making excuses for him.

"I get it," I tell him. "You don't want to pressure us to do what we're not capable of. Winning isn't that important. The main thing is to put in a good effort."

All eyes are on the coach, who has that odd habit of tilting his head while he's thinking something over.

"That's incorrect, Rosalie," he finally replies. "The goal of any competitive sport is to win. And this should be accomplished by exploiting every possible advantage—physical, mental, and strategic."

We regard each other in confusion. Where did *that* come from out of a clear blue sky? And if he really believes it, where has he been for half a game while we were out there getting murdered?

We switch sides for the second half, but that's the only thing different about it. The Seahawks put their starters back in, and before you know it, they're stampeding down the field, and the ball's in our net again.

And just as quickly, Coach Aidact is off our bench. He covers the distance to the umpire in four humongous strides. "No goal! The ball rolled out of bounds during the rush along the sidelines!"

The ump stands his ground. "Off the field, Coach!" he barks. "The ball was in bounds all the way! The call is a good goal!"

"The call is wrong!" Mr. Aidact insists. "The ball

was outside the line for more than a third of a second." He stalks over to the boundary. "Right here. You can see where the chalk is scuffed."

"You're pushing your luck, Coach!" the man warns.

Mr. Aidact is not going to be bullied. "Change the call."

"Call's already been made, pal!"

"The call is wrong! I know it with one hundred percent certainty—pal."

The ump is getting really steamed. "I'm not your pal! In fact, I'm starting to lose my patience with you!"

Uncomfortable glances pass between our players. What's Coach Aidact doing? Doesn't he see how angry the ump is getting?

Mr. Aidact stalks so close to the man that the two are practically nose to nose. "How can I make you understand that it's impossible for me to be mistaken about this?"

"That's it!" the umpire bellows. *"You're gone!"*

"Don't be ridiculous," Mr. Aidact replies. "I'm right here."

"Don't sass me!" the man thunders. "I'm throwing you out. If you don't leave the field right now, you forfeit the game with the score six–nothing against you."

"Five–nothing," the coach corrects.

"Out!"

And when Mr. Aidact heads for the bleachers, the umpire points to the exit. *"All* the way out! You can wait for your team in the parking lot. And I'll be sure to shoot your principal an email about the great example you're setting for your players."

We're just standing there while our coach is exiled from the game. I don't know what to think. On the one hand, he never did any coaching, not for a second. On the other, he was trying to stick up for us. And for that, they kicked him out. It makes me mad.

Mr. Perkins is hurrying across the field after the coach, lugging that big briefcase full of tools.

The umpire stops him. "Where do you think you're going?"

"I have to stay with him—"

"Is there another coach?" the ump demands.

The student teacher actually looks around. I can't tell you why. We didn't come with anybody else.

"Uh—no," he admits.

"Then this is your team. Let's get on with it."

That's how we end up with a coach who wouldn't know field hockey from ballroom dancing. His nervous attention is on the parking lot—and we soon understand why. Before our astonished eyes, Mr. Aidact climbs onto the hood of our school bus, throws up a leg, and hoists himself onto the roof. There he stands, straight as an antenna, his gaze riveted on our field.

The umpire shakes his head in disbelief. "What's the matter with that darn fool? We're going to have to scrape him off the pavement with a putty knife."

"He's not a fool," I say defensively. "He's our coach, and he cares about us."

"And if he says that ball was out," Cassidy adds, "I believe him."

The umpire sighs. "Let's just get this game over with."

"Like it's not over already," I hear the opposing captain sneer, to a chorus of snickers from the Seahawks. They're pointing at Mr. Aidact and laughing like he's some sort of clown.

It bugs me. Just because we stink and our coach is perched on the roof of a bus doesn't mean we're a joke.

So we start playing again, with us down six–zip. But something's different now. We're ticked off, aggressive, running harder. Every time a Seahawk touches the ball, there's a Bobcat right in her face. And instead of carving us up with those pinpoint passes of theirs, our opponents are backing up. Pretty soon they start making mistakes, and we have possession almost as often as they do.

They're still better than us, but when they go on the attack, we stand right up to them. To be honest, I think we're just mad. Partly because of what happened to our coach, and partly because who died and left them queen?

The next time Captain Linebacker comes at me, I plant myself directly in her path and hold my ground. She might bulldoze me, but she'd better know that pain is a two-way street, and I intend to pass out my share to the people who laughed at our coach.

Her eyes widen in surprise and she hesitates just for a second. That's when I make my move. I aim my stick like a pool cue and deftly poke the ball away from her. I'm so stunned that it works that I'm lost for an instant. I take in the game around me—players from both teams, frozen in time, and far upfield, Cassidy, just outside the Seahawks' sixteen-yard circle, with no defender anywhere near her.

What to do? The answer comes from the parking lot. In a voice so loud that it sounds like it's being broadcast over a loudspeaker, Mr. Aidact delivers his coaching instruction:

"*Pa-a-a-a-ss!!!*"

Leaning in for extra power, I crouch down low and blast a pass with all my might. It sails in a graceful arc, bounces once, and clicks onto Cassidy's stick. It doesn't stay there for long. As desperate defenders, caught out of position, converge from all directions, Cassidy dashes in on the goalkeeper and sends the ball into the top right corner of the net.

It's our first goal as a team. And even though we're getting killed, it's a magic moment. As we celebrate at midfield, we look to the parking lot, and Coach Aidact—still atop the bus—punches the air in triumph. I can't quite explain why, but nothing has ever made me feel more proud.

When play resumes, it's a whole different game, and the Bobcats are in command. I can't even explain why. It's like aliens abducted our entire team and replaced us with real field hockey players. No, scratch that. We're still ourselves. We're just so *motivated* that we run all over the Seahawks. We beat them to every loose ball. When they do have possession, our sticks are everywhere, probing, grabbing, checking.

And scoring. Cassidy adds a second goal. And pretty soon after that, Darcy Jimenez slips a low shot underneath their goalie, narrowing the Seahawks' lead to 6–3. Mr. Aidact waves his approval from atop the bus.

We pretty much have to coach ourselves, since Mr. Perkins is a dead loss. He paces along the sidelines, clutching his briefcase to his heart and staring at the parking lot. We handle our own substitutions. It's actually easier than it sounds because we're running so hard. When we get to the point where we're too gassed to put one foot in front of the other, we stagger to the sidelines to be replaced by fresh blood.

I never go off—not even once. When I start to feel tired, I just glance over the fence, and there he is, our loyal coach, watching us fight, even though the odds are stacked against us.

At first the Seahawks are rocked back on their heels. Then they start to get frustrated. As we sprint past them, they reach out with their sticks, tripping and spearing in an attempt to slow us down. Again and again, the whistle sounds. I'll never forgive that jerk umpire for banishing our coach, but I have to give him credit. He's fair, and calls fouls when he sees them. Cassidy, who has a deadly shot, converts two penalty corners into goals. And before you know it, Brightling has narrowed the lead to 6–5.

My eyes stay riveted to the scoreboard clock. Exactly 1:19 remains in the game.

I normally keep a low profile on the team. All the seventh graders do. We leave the leadership roles to the veterans like Cassidy and Leticia. But I can't help myself.

"Stop it!" I snap. "Stop cheering! Yeah, we've had a

great comeback—but it's all for nothing if we can't finish it off!"

"Lighten up, Rosalie," Ainsley advises. "We've got five goals. Judging by the first half, I thought we'd get zero."

I gesture toward the parking lot, where Mr. Aidact stands like a sentry, watching our every move. "Is the coach lightening up? I don't think so. Remember what he told us? The goal of any competitive sport is to *win*. Which means six to five might as well be fifty to zip."

"She's right," Cassidy decides. "Let's tie this up—for Coach Aidact."

"For the coach," Leticia agrees, and we all bump fists.

When the Seahawks bring up the ball, it's obvious that the game has changed one more time. The team that dominated us for the entire first half is back, and they're determined to hang on to their narrow lead. Our attackers and midfielders go after them, sticks reaching, digging, probing for a steal, but no luck.

Our opponents are playing keep-away, running out the clock, not even trying to score.

With a determination I never knew I had in me, I take off after Captain Linebacker, following her past midfield, deep into Seahawks' territory.

"You're out of position!" Cassidy shouts at me.

I don't answer. I can't—I'm saving every single ounce of breath for pure speed. Instead, I point to the scoreboard clock as it ticks under twenty-five seconds.

Cassidy joins the chase, but our opponent avoids us at every turn.

Fifteen seconds . . . ten . . .

Cassidy makes a desperation lunge for the ball, and when Captain Linebacker twirls away from her, I pluck it right off her stick. The goalie comes out to cut down my angle as I blaze into the circle.

"*Sho-o-o-ot!!!*" comes a howl from the parking lot.

Five seconds . . . four . . . three . . .

I use my shoulders to aim, just like the coach taught us in practice. The shot is dead-on, but at the last instant, the goalie kicks out and gets a pad in front of it.

Disappointment shatters me, and I crumple to the grass. *I missed! How could I miss?*

Almost in slow motion, Cassidy's stick rounds into my field of vision. It catches the rebound in midair and slams it into the net just before the clock expires.

The comeback is complete. Tie game, 6–6.

It usually nauseates me when guys lose their minds over some sports play. I take it all back. The Bobcats go full dogpile on Cassidy and me. For a second, I'm convinced the screaming is going to bust my eardrums—and I'm doing at least half of it. Shaking each other like rag dolls, we scramble to our feet and stand there, facing the parking lot. But Mr. Aidact is gone.

"What happened to the coach?" Leticia blurts.

Then we see him—in full flight, leaping over the fence that surrounds the field. He hits the ground running and pounds across the turf at a speed an Olympic sprinter would envy. He barrels right into our midst, leaping up and down along with our celebration. He's saying something, but we're so loud that we can't make out what it is. He keeps repeating it, so we quiet down to hear these words of wisdom from our coach.

He's *singing*!

"We are the champions, my friends . . .
And we'll keep on fighting till the end. . . ."

Mr. Aidact sure is full of surprises.

"I'd like a word with you, Mr. Aidact." Mr. Perkins tries to separate the coach from us, but he can't get into our circle. He won't put down his briefcase, and we keep bumping it away.

Next to join our celebration is our one and only fan,

Mom. She screams, "What a game!" spreads her arms wide, and delivers a big hug to . . . Mr. Aidact!

Not her own daughter. The coach. Sheesh!

It's disgusting, but I don't let it spoil the triumph of the moment. I only joined this team so it could look good on my record. Now, thanks to Coach Aidact, I'm a Bobcat till I die!

CONFIDENTIAL REPORT

To: Department of Education, Washington, DC
From: Paul Perkins, PE
Project: AIDACT

Teachers at Brightling Middle School continue to dump unwanted tasks on AIDACT, and AIDACT, for obvious reasons, is tireless. AIDACT's ability to adapt to new situations is proving to be even better than we expected. However, there is a possible downside. AIDACT picks up enthusiasm observed from others and sometimes overdoes it. (See attached document: complaint from field hockey umpire.) Also, because AIDACT absorbs so much so quickly, singing and/or rapping is becoming a concern.

PROJECT STATUS: Green

SPECIAL EXPENSES
Repairs to dented roof of school bus

Steinke Newhouse

Detention sure isn't what it used to be.

It used to be just Mia Spinelli and me pretending to do homework and putting in time. It was punishment, but it also kind of wasn't. At least we had the satisfaction that some poor teacher had to stick around babysitting us, hating it even worse than we did.

What a difference a few weeks make. Oh, sure, Mia's still here—and *always* me. But instead of a new teacher every day, we have Aidact and Perkins. And since the faculty aren't all sharing detention duty anymore, they're throwing the kitchen sink at Mr. Aidact. Every kid who breaks the tiniest little rule gets sent to room 233 at dismissal, so it's *crowded*. Some days it's practically a mob scene and they have to bring in extra chairs. What's next, huh? A bouncer at the door, with a red carpet and a velvet rope?

I miss the old days.

Today's the worst. It's so packed that we have to double up at the desks. And just as I'm settling in to not do homework, things get rowdy on the other side of the room, with a dozen hands in the air and kids shouting out the names of cities in Asia, like Shanghai, Tokyo, and Hong Kong.

"What the hey?" Mia, my desk-mate, complains.

I wave Mr. Aidact over. "There's no yelling in detention," I inform him. He's still new, so maybe he doesn't know.

"Oh, that's not yelling," he replies. "That's the Trivia Club."

I'm amazed. "The whole Trivia Club got detention?" They seem like a bunch of goody-goodies, heavy on the sixth graders. Sixth graders always aim to please. Except me, but I wasn't your average sixth grader.

"I'm their faculty adviser," he exclaims. "They meet at the same time as detention, so it has to be here."

That's partly my fault. I told Kevin Krumlich that Mr. Aidact knows any song lyric you can think of. Turns out Krumlich has a big mouth—I mean planet-size. Pretty soon there was a rumor going around that the new teacher is unstumpable and it became a game to try to stump him. I don't get how that turned into a club, but I don't get a lot of things, just like I don't get why people can't pronounce my name.

"They're horning in on our thing," I complain.

"Their thing can be your thing," the teacher invites. "Join our trivia quiz."

"Quiz," I repeat dubiously. "That sounds a lot like school."

"Trivia is fun," Mr. Aidact explains. "And it keeps the mind sharp and engaged."

"Yeah, but the questions are too boring," I argue. "They never ask important stuff, like what rapper died on December eighth, 2019."

And just like that, the hands shoot up again, and the trivia kids are shouting answers to my question

"Wrong!" I bray. "It was Juice Wrld! Ha—in your face!"

And instead of being mad at me, they laugh and even clap a little. Nobody's ever clapped at anything *I* said before.

"You should join the Trivia Club," Mr. Aidact advises.

"I can't join a club!" I snap at him. "I have detention?"

"Trivia Club *is* detention," Mia reasons. "At least, they're in the same place."

And that's how I end up a member of my very first club. We're going to get our own page in the yearbook. Can you believe that? Me in a yearbook. According to Mr. Aidact, a photographer is going to come and take our picture for it.

"Okay, but if they put me down as Stinky, I quit," I grumble.

Mr. Aidact looks mystified. "Why would they do that? Your name is completely different."

That's the best thing about Mr. Aidact. Even when he's lying, it feels good to believe him.

✶

Mia is the closest thing to a friend that I have in this school, since we spend so much time together in detention. But I have trouble understanding her sometimes.

"He says he dumped me, but I dumped him first!"

I don't think that can be the answer to question 12 of the trivia quiz, which is about exoplanets, whatever they are.

"Who?" I ask.

"Darryl Yarmolenko!"

I know Darryl. Everybody does. He's the captain of the basketball team. We've come up together since elementary school, although he mostly ignores me now. He's popular and I'm me.

"What?" Her eyes narrow. "You don't believe me?"

I shrug. "I didn't know you had a boyfriend."

"*Ex*-boyfriend!" she snarls. "And I dumped him, just so you know!"

I never wanted to know.

The next time I see Darryl, it's in the gym before school. He's shooting baskets, and there's an adult with him—his dad. The thing is, every time Darryl misses, Mr. Yarmolenko dumps all over him—"Your form is wrong! . . . I've seen better wrist action on an old lady sipping tea! . . . You'll never make the high school team unless you pull your socks up!"

Darryl's face is bright red. You can tell that his father is making him feel like a cockroach who got stepped on and refuses to lie down and die. To be honest, I feel bad for the guy, even though he's a sports star who normally wouldn't bother wiping his sneakers on me.

That's when Mr. Aidact and Mr. Perkins enter through the door to the parking lot.

Mr. Aidact approaches the pair. "I think that's enough coaching for today."

Darryl's dad doesn't look away from adjusting the position of his son's hands on the ball. "We're working here, buddy."

"I don't think it's helpful to put too much pressure on him," the teacher persists. "The focus should be on—"

Mr. Yarmolenko cuts him off. "*I'll* be the judge of what we should be focusing on. He's my kid!"

Mr. Aidact doesn't even blink. "Yes, but he's *my* pupil."

"It's okay, Dad—" Darryl begins.

His father wheels on Mr. Aidact. "Have you ever sunk a basket in your life?"

"I have not," the teacher admits.

"Figures." Mr. Yarmolenko drops the basketball and starts for the exit. "Everybody's an expert. This isn't over, Darryl!" he tosses back at his son.

Mr. Aidact picks up the ball and turns it over in his hands. "Seems simple enough." He takes a set shot and misses by two feet.

Darryl's father laughs out loud. "What did I tell you?"

Mr. Aidact tries again. Another air ball.

"You don't have to do this, Mr. Aidact," Darryl mumbles.

"Sure, he does," Mr. Yarmolenko jeers from the doorway. "These teachers act like they know everything, but what have they ever accomplished in the real world?"

The next attempt rattles off the rim.

"Go ahead, LeBron!"

And the fourth try—swish.

"Pure luck," calls Mr. Yarmolenko.

Here's the thing. Mr. Aidact keeps on shooting and never misses again. From close in. From far out. Even from half court. Nothing but net.

Darryl is wide-eyed. "Mr. Aidact—you could make the Lakers!"

The teacher has hit fourteen in a row by the time Mr. Yarmolenko slinks out of the gym, scowling. He buries two more before the bell rings.

Mr. Aidact returns the ball to the rack. "It's a physics problem. Force, trajectory, arc, gravity." He disappears down the hall, with Perkins hustling behind him with that big briefcase.

I guess I'm standing there with my mouth hanging open, because Darryl shoots me a scowl. "What are you looking at, Stinky?"

It might be the first time he's spoken to me since elementary school.

I don't give him a hard time for messing up my name. I saw him getting bullied by his jerk dad, and that's something you can't unsee.

"That was good timing," I offer. "You know, Mr. Aidact arriving right when he did."

"Big deal," Darryl mutters.

I kind of know what he means. Yeah, Mr. Aidact came to his defense. But when Darryl gets home from school today, Mr. Aidact isn't going to be there.

Although Darryl and I aren't friends, I rack my brain for a piece of advice that might help him. I may be below him in every way, but one problem I *don't* have is a jerk dad.

Finally, I've got it. "I think you should get a detention as soon as possible."

Oliver Zahn

Sitting in detention gives a guy time to think.
And sitting in detention with Mr. Aidact gives a guy a
lot to think *about*.

"I mean, why are we here?" I whisper to Nathan,
who's serving detention at the desk next to mine.

"Why?" He practically does a spit take. "Have you
forgotten that little business with the Big Wheel? Or
the costume change that was supposed to be foolproof?"

"It *was* foolproof," I insist. "I'd bet my reputation
as a rule-wrecker on it. Could one teacher in a thousand have identified my Batman suit from a tiny thread?
Could one in a *million*?"

"Too bad Mr. Aidact is one in a *billion*," he says bitterly.

I nod. "He's been all over me since the first spitball of the year! And the stunt with the toy cars—not only did he figure it out, but he instantly knew who to pin it on."

Nathan shrugs. "It was only a matter of time before a teacher came along who had your number."

I fold my arms in front of my chest. "I refuse to believe it. There's something off about that guy. He knows things that are impossible to know."

"He's unreal," Nathan agrees. "There's nothing we can do about it."

Typical Nathan. I love the kid, but he's happy to drift along like a twig floating downstream. He doesn't care whether he controls his own destiny. He probably doesn't even think about it.

Lucky for him, he's got me as a best friend.

"There's always something you can do about it."

A Google search for the name Aidact churns up over three hundred thousand hits—and none of them are people.

"Really?" Nathan says in surprise. "Everybody's on the internet."

"Not Mr. Aidact," I conclude, sifting through the pages of links on my computer. "And I guess he doesn't have any relatives either."

Our investigation begins right after school on the floor of my room. Obviously, I can't go through all three hundred thousand, but the hits are mostly government things—bills and laws called the something-or-other Aid Act. Real boring stuff.

"Maybe you should try to find his address," Nathan suggests. "He might not be on Google, but everybody has to live somewhere."

Not Mr. Aidact. According to the online directory, there's no one by that name in our town, the state, or the entire country. We try a few other internet resources, with the same results. Ditto the major social media sites. Nothing. We even look in the old-fashioned phone book my dad keeps around. No Aidacts.

I'm starting to get frustrated. "What's the deal with this guy? It's like he doesn't even exist!"

"He exists, all right," Nathan says grimly. "Seems to me we've been serving a lot of detention thanks to *somebody*—and his boomer student teacher."

"That's it!" My spirits soar. "Perkins! He drives Mr. Aidact to school every day, and drives him back home again. If we can find out where Perkins lives, we can ride there on our bikes in the morning and follow him when he goes to pick up Mr. Aidact."

"What if he commutes from forty miles away?" Nathan challenges.

I shrug. "One way to find out."

Googling Perkins presents the opposite problem. If there are no Aidacts, there are Perkinses up the wazoo. We do searches on everybody, ruling people out one by one, until we find our student teacher: Paul Perkins, 1342 Larch Street—a small apartment complex about half a mile from school.

We put our plan into action the very next morning. My mother seems pretty suspicious when she catches me slipping my bike out of the garage at seven thirty so Nathan and I can "head in early to work on a project."

Her eyes narrow. "What happened to 'being in school more than five seconds before the late bell is a waste of precious youth'?"

I hate it when Mom uses my brilliance against me. "That was a sixth-grade thing," I tell her. "I'm way more mature now. Education is important."

The look on her face plainly says she isn't buying it, but she doesn't stop me as I ride off. I'm joined by Nathan at the corner, and we pedal away together for Larch Street.

We stash our bikes at the edge of the complex and continue on foot.

"How do we know which apartment is his?" Nathan asks.

"Simple." It takes just a few seconds to locate the white Prius. It's parked in space 23, a short walk from a bright green door bearing the same number. "Right there."

At that very moment, the door starts to open. Hurriedly, we duck into some bushes and wait for Perkins to emerge.

And someone does step out of the unit onto the front walk. But it's not our student teacher. It's Mr. Aidact.

Nathan's brow furrows. "If Mr. Aidact lives here," he whispers, "how come the place is under Perkins's name?"

I can only shrug.

From our spot in the bushes, we can see into the apartment and down the hall. We watch, transfixed as a door opens and another figure steps out of the nearer of two bedrooms—skinny, slight, and lugging a large briefcase. Perkins.

"They're *roommates*?" I breathe.

The two teachers lock the apartment behind them, get into the Prius, and drive off in the direction of school.

We stay in the bushes for a few minutes after they go.

My mind is whirling. "Okay, okay. I didn't see this coming."

"It sort of makes sense," Nathan reasons. "Student teachers don't get paid. Maybe Perkins is bunking with Mr. Aidact to save money."

"Maybe," I concede. "Except that it's *Perkins*'s apartment. So it's not Perkins bunking with Aidact. It's the other way around. You know what's under Aidact's name? Nothing! Not even Mr. Aidact!"

"Calm down," Nathan soothes as we head over to where we stashed the bikes. "We wanted to know where Mr. Aidact lives and now we do. It isn't what we expected, but at least it's over."

"It's just starting," I correct him. "We're going to get to the bottom of this if it's the last thing we do."

He grimaces. "I hate when you use that word."

I pick my bike up off the grass. "What word?"

"*We*."

✳

At school, whenever I see Mr. Aidact and Mr. Perkins, my brain threatens to boil over. In homeroom; in algebra; in the cafeteria, where Mr. Aidact is on lunch duty; and at three thirty in detention, my mind works double speed, sifting through all the information I have about

Brightling's staff newbie and his middle-aged student teacher:

- ✦ Perkins never lets Aidact out of his sight. When Aidact runs field hockey practice, Perkins watches from the window of the detention room, making notes.
- ✦ Perkins eats lunch, but Aidact always skips. Aidact is never seen with so much as a water bottle, coffee cup, or any form of snack.
- ✦ The two live together, arrive together, and leave together. Perkins always drives.
- ✦ The apartment and car belong to Perkins. The name Aidact appears nowhere, not even on the list of faculty on the school's website.
- ✦ Considering he's a student teacher, Perkins hasn't taught a single lesson, or even a single word.

What does it mean? Wild ideas flash around my head. Each one provides a partial explanation, but nothing explains it all. What if Mr. Aidact is the real student teacher and the boomer is his supervisor? Then their ages would make perfect sense, and so would their behavior—Aidact teaching and Perkins making notes. But if that's true, why bother telling everybody it's the other way around? And why would Mr. Aidact be the only student teacher at Brightling who needs an outside supervisor?

If Perkins isn't a student teacher, what is he? A chauffeur? Why would a middle school teacher have a chauffeur—especially a live-in chauffeur? Could there be more to it than that? Like maybe Perkins is his bodyguard? But why would a teacher need one of those? What is he afraid of? Unless Mr. Aidact isn't a teacher at all. He's the exiled prince of some tiny, obscure country where Aidact is as common a name as Smith or Jones. Only that doesn't answer the biggest question of all: What self-respecting prince would move into a dinky apartment and teach seventh grade?

After school, Nathan and I bike together back to my house. I get the impression that he wants to drop our investigation, at least for now. It's been a long day, and I'm tired too. But there's no way I'm going to let this slide, not even till tomorrow. If we don't get some answers pronto, I'm not going to be able to live with myself.

He waits outside while I go into the garage and riffle through a box of my old toys. There it is, under the

Thomas trains and the Lincoln Logs—my periscope. I never really found a use for it except to spy up on high shelves when I was trying to find where Mom was hiding the Christmas presents. I think I got it when I was about six. Who could have predicted that it would finally come in handy after all these years?

"You're kidding," Nathan tells me when I show it to him.

I get it. The periscope is bright blue plastic and there's a sticker all the way up the length of it that says SUBMARINE COMMANDER along with the picture of a clear-eyed naval officer in the crosshairs of a circle. "So it's babyish. So what? Would you rather get caught with your big nose pressed up against Mr. Aidact's window?"

"Don't drop it," he warns as we climb back on our bikes.

At 1342 Larch Street, we replay our actions from this morning, stashing our bikes and hiding in the bushes opposite apartment 23. One problem: this time, the Prius isn't parked in its spot.

"We wait," I decide.

"But what if they went to a movie?" Nathan complains. "What if they're driving to Atlanta to visit dear old Aunt Aidact?"

"There is no Aunt Aidact," I reason. "Otherwise she

would have turned up in the Google search. Maybe field hockey practice ran late or something."

It's really only about twenty minutes, but when you're crouched in the bushes getting scratched by branches and listening to your best friend whining, it feels like years.

Finally, the Prius pulls into space 23, and the two teachers get out. Mr. Aidact carries five big grocery bags. Perkins carries the briefcase and nothing else.

"Considering they're together every minute," Nathan whispers, "they never say a word to each other."

I wait for them to enter the apartment. Then I count ten Mississippis and climb out of the bushes, hauling Nathan behind me. We drop to the grass and, staying low, slither up to the big picture window. The curtains are closed, but there's a gap of about three inches in the middle—an ideal vulnerability to be exploited by a Submarine Commander periscope. Carefully, I telescope the top of the toy above the window ledge and take my first look inside.

It works perfectly. Okay, the mirrors are a little dusty, but I can see everything. The living room has a fireplace, and across the mantel is a collection of Chia Pets in various stages of sprouting. There's a pass-through to the kitchen, where Mr. Aidact, now wearing a T-shirt, is unloading tins of soup and, for some reason, three cans of WD-40 lubricating oil, like my dad uses on the door when it squeaks. I've never looked into a teacher's house before, but I definitely wasn't expecting that. I mean, how many squeaky doors can they have?

When he's finished putting away the groceries, Mr. Aidact steps out into the living room and stands there, motionless. There's no sign of his roommate.

"What's happening?" Nathan whispers nervously.

"Nothing."

"How could it be nothing?"

I squirm aside to give him a turn at the periscope.

"You're right," he says finally. "It *is* nothing. Why's he just *standing* there? Doesn't he want to sit down?"

I shrug and take back the viewing spot. Watching somebody who doesn't move a muscle—doesn't even blink—is exhausting for some reason. And *weird* doesn't even begin to explain it. I'm almost ready to scream when Mr. Perkins walks into the room and sets the briefcase down on the coffee table. He circles the unmoving Mr. Aidact, looking him over like a customer inspecting a used car he's thinking of buying. He brushes some lint off Mr. Aidact's shoulder, nods to himself, and bends down to open the case on the table beside him.

It's my first glimpse inside the famous briefcase. And

whatever I was expecting, this isn't it. It's some kind of toolbox, filled with gleaming silver instruments.

A doctor? Like he's Mr. Aidact's personal physician? My mind circles back to the exiled prince theory. But then Mr. Perkins takes out one of the instruments, and there's no question about what it is: a tiny precision wrench.

What's that for? I wonder. *What's he going to fix?* And before that thought has fully formed in my mind, I have my answer. He reaches out and sticks the wrench right into the underside of Mr. Aidact's forearm.

I wait for Mr. Aidact to cry out or pull away. But he remains still as a statue. And if that sounds bonkers, keep your seat belts fastened, because it only gets nuttier from here: with his thumb and forefinger, Perkins twists the wrench and Mr. Aidact's left forearm pops open like a lunch box, hanging there on a hinge. And inside the arm?

I gawk. I goggle.

No blood. No bone. No muscle tissue. It looks like the inside of a computer—wires, circuits, silicon chips. I watch, my spine freezing into a column of ice, as Perkins selects another instrument that looks like a dental pick and begins making adjustments to the machinery in there.

Nathan is tugging on my jacket. "What is it? What do you see?"

Wordlessly, I let him take my place at the viewfinder. He watches for a few seconds and then pulls away, his eyes as wide as dinner plates. "An artificial arm?" he whispers.

"I—I guess so." But I get back to the periscope just in time to see Perkins open up the *other* forearm! "Make that—*two* artificial arms," I murmur in a reedy tone.

"No!"

It doesn't end there. Mr. Aidact rolls up his pant leg and the little wrench unlocks a panel that covers the entire left calf. More electronics. More machinery.

I move aside. "Take a look at this."

Nathan shakes his head. "I don't want to."

Next comes a small panel on the stomach, followed by one on the back of the neck. Perkins works delicately with several different tools, fiddling, tightening, and making adjustments. An air puffer clears away dust particles. Every moving panel gets a small spritz of WD-40 before it gets closed up again. Finally, Perkins connects a laptop computer over the left shoulder blade. A timing wheel whirls on the screen as a progress indicator rises to 100 percent.

Even in the cool afternoon, I find myself sweating like

a hog. Droplets of perspiration sting my eyes, but I can't look away from what's happening inside apartment 23.

Reluctantly, Nathan takes another peek into the viewfinder and comes away shaking his head. "What does it *mean*?"

There can only be one answer to that question, but forcing the words out of my mouth causes genuine physical pain:

"Our teacher isn't human."

Nathan Popova

"This isn't happening!" The Oliver Alert is an unin-terrupted earsplitting screech, but this goes far beyond my partner in crime getting me in trouble. "I woke up this morning a normal kid and now—now look what you made me see!"

In answer, Oliver pulls the periscope out of the window and flattens both of us to the ground. Lying there, my cheek pressed into an anthill, I peer up out of the corner of my eye just in time to see Perkins gazing out through the gap in the curtains. All he has to do is glance down, and there we are.

A fat ant crawls up my cheek, but I don't dare brush

it away for fear of attracting the student teacher's attention. At such close range, it looks like a giant alien. Why, oh why, do I let Oliver drag me into things?

Perkins stands there for what seems like an impossibly long time. Then he pulls the curtains completely closed.

Oliver and I don't wait for an engraved invitation. We scramble away so fast that we forget the periscope, and Oliver has to crawl back to get it. If Mr. Aidact can identify a Batman suit from one thread, he could probably sequence our DNA from the viewfinder of the toy.

He. The pronoun sticks in my mind. Is Mr. Aidact a he? The last time I checked, it looked like he was some kind of machine!

We sprint all the way to our bikes, jump on, and pedal away at top speed. "You know in spy movies," I pant to Oliver riding beside me, "where they talk about information being on a need-to-know basis? Well, that was something I *never needed to know!*"

Even Oliver seems pretty shaken by what we've just seen. "I get it. I had some pretty weird ideas about Mr. Aidact, but this is the last thing I expected!"

We pedal as if we don't know or care where we're going. Away from 1342 Larch Street is enough of a destination. You can't keep riding forever, though. So eventually, I fall in behind Oliver and let him take the lead. It's my fatal flaw: following my best friend. I complain about the stuff he gets me into, but it's my own fault. I have an Oliver Alert, but what good does it do me? I hear it; I get stressed-out by it; I never pay attention to its warning. When it comes to Oliver, I go where I'm dragged.

In this case, I'm dragged to my very own house because "your Wi-Fi is faster than mine."

"What's Wi-Fi got to do with the fact that our teacher has circuits instead of guts?" I ask.

"The first time we googled *Aidact*, we were looking for a *person*," Oliver reasons, leaning his bike against the side of my garage. "We hadn't seen—you know—what we just saw."

"Which is what, exactly?" I demand. "Because if you tell me, we'll both know."

"That's what research is for," he reasons. "We can't be sure of anything yet, but it's pretty obvious Mr. Aidact isn't your average middle school teacher."

"But is he a *machine*?" I probe.

"We have to keep our minds open. The only thing we know is that he isn't human. Humans don't have wires and microchips under their skin."

Oliver's right that the Wi-Fi at my house really is

faster. So as soon as we're up in my room, we put that Wi-Fi to work on our phones.

We don't have time to go through all three hundred thousand links for *Aidact*, so we try to narrow down our search by adding extra keywords—*Aidact* plus *Perkins*; *Aidact* plus *Brightling*; *Aidact* plus *human*; *Aidact* plus *electronic*; *Aidact* plus *machine*. We spend hours clicking on side links and getting nowhere.

Then I try a combination neither of us has thought of: *Aidact* plus *teacher*.

The first link that comes up takes us to an article from *Educator's Digest*, summer 2018:

DEPARTMENT OF EDUCATION SHELVES "AIDACT" PROJECT

According to a spokesperson, the Department of Education will be giving up on its ambitious AIDACT project. The goal of AIDACT—which stands for Artificially Intelligent Designated Android Classroom Teacher—was to place convincingly human robotic teachers in classrooms across the country. . . .

Robotic! That's the word we've been dancing around ever since the periscope showed us what was going on inside apartment 23. Our teacher is a robot!

"A robot!" Oliver nods so violently that I'm afraid his head might snap off and roll across the carpet. "How could we miss it?"

"Oh, I don't know," I retort in exasperation. "Maybe because real life isn't Star Wars?"

"But this is *exactly* Mr. Aidact," he insists. "A convincingly human robot. If it wasn't for us, I'll bet nobody ever would have figured it out!"

According to the article, AIDACT units would be placed in test schools. Faculty and school employees would be informed, but the larger community—including the students—would know nothing. Part of the experiment was to see if the robot teachers could pass as the real thing.

"No wonder he caught my spitball!" Oliver breathes. "I told you that was impossible! But he has superhuman reaction time!"

"And listen to this," I add, reading ahead on my phone. "'Each AIDACT unit was to be accompanied by a Department of Education project engineer.'"

"Perkins!" Oliver explodes. "I knew he couldn't be a student teacher! And it explains why they live together and Perkins does all the driving and watches over him twenty-four-seven."

"It explains everything," I agree. "Only—according

to *Educator's Digest*, Project AIDACT got scrapped back in 2018. So how come we've got a real AIDACT and his engineer in our homeroom?"

We read on. The article says that the AIDACTs were expected to be a little stiff and unnatural at first, but their built-in AI systems would learn from the people around them, training the units to become more "human" every day. The project was stopped because the AI technology was not advanced enough to respond to changing classroom situations and to meet diverse student needs.

I frown. "When you think about it, that's the kind of thing Mr. Aidact is best at. He trashed a whole classroom so I'd understand ratios. The trivia kids think he's a genius because he knows all the answers. The field hockey girls would walk through fire for him. And even real oddballs like Stinky and Mia love him. Not a single teacher in this town has known what to do with Stinky since kindergarten, and Mr. Aidact has him eating out of his hand."

"That must be it," Oliver decides. "Back in 2018, the AI wasn't good enough, so they had to cancel the project. But now it's better, so they started it up again."

"And we got a teacher with a computer brain that always knows who to blame when things get screwy,"

I comment bitterly. "Think about the prank with the cars—Mr. Aidact figured it out because he has the whole internet inside his head."

Oliver nods. "That must be where he gets his song lyrics and his trivia. He's like a walking Google."

"It's kind of scary," I say with a shiver. "Our teacher has *powers*, like one of the Avengers!"

"He's not so great," Oliver scoffs. "Mr. Aidact may have a super-brain, but you know what he doesn't have? A sense of humor. If you can't find things funny, you're not smart. And no AI is going to teach you."

I sigh. "So what happens now? Who do we tell about this?"

"Are you kidding? Haven't you ever heard that knowledge is power? We know something nobody else does! We have to hang on to that."

"Why?"

"Let's say Candiotti somehow figures out that we were the ones who disappeared her precious trophy. We're dead, right? But not if we mention the 'big news' we're thinking of spreading around town: there's a robot teacher at our school, and the principal's been hiding it from everybody."

I hold my head. "Now you've got us blackmailing the principal." My Oliver Alert offers up a few half-hearted clangs, but this news about Mr. Aidact makes everything else seem like small potatoes in comparison.

He grins. "It probably won't come to that. Besides, maybe Brightling has another field hockey trophy in our future."

"Fat chance," I retort. "We haven't been good since the seventies."

"Maybe not," he concedes. "But this year, we've got something no other team has: a robot coach with a computer brain."

Principal Candiotti

I could never regret choosing a career in educa-tion, but I make an exception when it comes to sitting on bleachers.

What designer of medieval torture chambers came up with the concept of perching for hours on cold metal, with zero back support, and your knees up around your chin?

It's fine for the kids—they're made of rubber. They don't even notice it. But when you get to be my age, you're not nearly so supple. Just try to hold yourself in these stress positions for an entire football game or soccer match or, my personal favorite, field hockey. You'll feel it in the gluteus maximus the next morning, I assure you.

Still, it's all worth it as our Cassidy Bonner splits two defenders and fires a deadly shot right between the goalkeeper's pads, increasing our lead to 5–2. So help me, I could get up and cheer—except my body would probably lock up and I might fall through the gap in the bleachers and never be seen again. If the Bobcats can hold on, this will be our fifth win in a row after that opening-day tie. I'm starting to get the feeling I thought I'd forgotten since the 1974 season, when *I* was the captain of the Lady Bobcats. These girls are special—there's no question about that. Cassidy with her blistering attack; Leticia, our stand-up goalie. Even some of our seventh graders are turning into solid players, especially Rosalie, whose height and long reach make her a natural defender.

I don't delude myself into believing they could be state championship material. For a school like Brightling, that's a once-in-a-lifetime thing. But it's nice to be winners again. I feel my brow darkening. I will never get over the loss of our trophy. It was so beautiful, so meaningful, and so irreplaceable. Why would anyone take it? It means nothing to a stranger, and everything to the pride of our school. I waited so long for someone to own up, or even to demand money for its return. But now I have to come to terms with the fact that it's gone forever.

"Nice shot, Ainsley!" It's 6–2.

"Oooh—cold!" Syesha Berg sits down beside me on the metal bleachers. "Are we winning?"

"Of course we're winning," I tell her impatiently. "That's what six to two means, Syesha. See the six is right below 'home'?" I don't mean to be rude. But I wish more of our teachers would take an interest in our sports teams.

"That's nice," she comments in her usual bland monotone. "I've been meaning to talk to you. About—*him.*"

"Him?"

"You know—Aidact."

I lower my voice. "Please call him *Mr.* Aidact when we're in public. I know what he is—we all do. But the school board expects us to keep that private."

"Well, all my boys have gone crazy because of him," she complains. "The poetry unit is a shambles. All they want to do is rap and recite lyrics. And when I ask where they're getting it, they all say Mr. Aidact."

"He comes straight from the Department of Education," I remind her. "It's a tremendous honor that Brightling was chosen for this project."

"I don't care," she insists. "He's a terrible influence on the kids."

"Are you talking about the singing?" Kelly Tapper takes the seat on the other side of me. "You can't teach a class anymore without hearing this constant mumbling. And you know they're all singing and rapping under their breath."

"You've both been teaching long enough to know a thing or two about kids and their obsessions," I chide them both. "Today it's singing; tomorrow they'll be dancing; next week they'll be playing with fidget spinners. Wait it out. It'll pass."

"It might never pass if Aidact keeps egging them on," Syesha complains.

"He's not egging them on," I explain patiently. "He's not capable of it. Paul Perkins explained everything. Mr. Aidact's AI is designed to learn from the people surrounding him. And at a middle school, that means kids. If the kids are interested in music, he picks that up and feeds it back to them. He's just programmed that way."

"Then it should be a simple thing for Paul or somebody else to program him a *different* way," Syesha insists.

"I don't hear either of you complaining when Mr. Aidact takes over your bus duty or your lunch duty or detention," I point out. "I can't remember the last time anybody else on staff had to cover outdoor recess at this school."

"As it should be," Syesha retorts. "We're real people, who can feel the cold, the wind, and the rain. He can't suffer from the elements any more than a car that's parked outside in the snow."

When I socialize with other principals, our favorite topic of conversation is how teachers are often pettier and more immature than students. My staff has no problem reaping the benefits of having an AIDACT unit to take over the dirty jobs. But when it comes to complaining about him, they have an awful lot to say.

I pause to cheer as Cassidy scores off a penalty corner to complete her hat trick. I had quite a few hat tricks myself in my playing days, so I know what a thrill it is. On the sidelines, Mr. Aidact is jumping up and down, high-fiving the girls, every bit as excited as the team. Correction—his AI system picks up on the girls' excitement and mirrors it. Not much like the robots from the old movies; he's not clanking along with his arms out in front of him—although Paul assures us that the moving parts have to be oiled and maintained like on any other mechanical device. But when you understand how the technology works, it makes perfect sense. And then the players see his reaction, which only acts as an amplifier for their own exhilaration. It's no wonder they adore him.

"I know it has its challenges," I concede. "But you have to admit it's a miracle from a scientific point of view. Look at him down there, coaching the girls. You'd never know he's"—I drop my voice to a whisper—"a *machine.*"

"I wish he was a machine," Syesha puts in grumpily. "A coffee machine. The Keurig in the faculty lounge has been broken for three weeks. How's the Department of Education at French roast?"

"The science teachers have a bone to pick with his Trivia Club," Kelly adds. "The kids can't tell the difference between real life and pop culture. In our test today, half my sixth graders thought the first person to walk on the moon was Han Solo."

There's a disturbance on the field. Mr. Aidact is in a spirited argument with the umpire, arms waving and lips flapping. The girls swarm around their coach, cheering their support.

"Now what?" Syesha groans. "I suppose he's late for his next oil change."

"Don't be unkind," I tell her. "He's disputing a questionable call—a stick foul on Rosalie."

Mr. Aidact's strident voice rings out, clear as a bell: "Anyone can see those sticks never touched! They were separated by a full two-point-five millimeters!"

I've asked Paul to turn down the volume on Mr. Aidact's audio output, but I guess he hasn't gotten around to it yet.

"Two-point-five millimeters," Kelly comments sarcastically. "Practically the Grand Canyon."

"You can't blame Mr. Aidact for noticing every little thing," I insist. "It may sound like nit-picking, but it's just how he's designed. And when he spots an officiating error, he disputes it, like any coach would."

The umpire signals to uphold the stick foul, and a frustrated Coach Aidact rips off his Bobcats hat and hurls it with all his might. Spinning like a flying saucer, the baseball cap sizzles across the field and buries itself brim-first in the trunk of a pine tree.

Syesha raises a plucked eyebrow. "Would any coach do *that*?"

I point down to the front row, where Paul Perkins is pounding the keyboard of his laptop. "Don't worry. Paul is already sending him a wireless command to dial it back."

As if on cue, Mr. Aidact retreats to the sidelines, still fuming. The girls cluster around him, dancing and exchanging high fives, even though his challenge was unsuccessful. Their coach stood up for his team, and that's what counts with them.

"Why doesn't Paul send him a wireless command to erase all those lyrics?" Syesha puts in sourly. "That would make *my* life a lot easier."

"It doesn't work that way. The command is just a suggestion. The AI system decides whether or not Mr. Aidact will follow it." I sigh. "Your frustrations are all understandable, but you have to remember what an honor it is that our school was chosen as a test site for the AIDACT project." I feel my face flush. "It's unfortunate that we have to keep it a secret for now. But one day, we'll get full credit for the groundbreaking work we're doing for the future of education."

I've already rehearsed the interview I'm going to give when *Educator's Digest* comes to take my picture for their cover. It's a great feather in my cap to be principal of the school where the very first AIDACT unit was launched. It'll be a cinch to get a superintendent's position after that.

"Groundbreaking," Syesha echoes morosely. "If they start making AIDACTs by the thousands, we'll all be out of a job."

"One of the movies in his trivia quiz is *The Matrix*," Kelly informs us. "You know—all humanity being taken over by machines?"

Syesha makes a face. "I'll bet it's his favorite film."

On the field, the final whistle signifies another big win for the Bobcats. I raise my aching hind end off the cold, hard bleachers and stand up to applaud the victors.

I watch as Mr. Aidact celebrates with the girls and accepts the congratulations of the opposing coach. I can't help wondering: Could Syesha be right? Will sophisticated robots from the Department of Education one day replace teachers?

And in some dark, movie-like future, will they eventually create an AIDACT unit capable of replacing a principal?

19

Rosalie Arnette

To succeed in the future, you have to be smart, focused, hardworking, and tough, but it also helps to have connections. And there's no better connection at Brightling than Avalon Pappas, editor in chief of the Brightling *Barker*, our school paper.

If there's an eighth grader I admire more than Cassidy, it has to be her. Avalon's going places—in high school, college, and beyond.

She runs the *Barker*'s basement office like a real newsroom, complete with reporters, feature writers, photographers, and designers who create the paper's layout every week on our iPad Pros.

I know most middle school papers are kind of boring, with articles about what the recycling club is doing, and how the bricks outside the library have to be tuck-pointed, whatever that is. But Avalon believes in hard-hitting journalism. Like the last editorial she wrote: she said whoever rode the Big Wheel on that video from the seventh-grade chat must know what happened to the missing field hockey trophy. Principal Candiotti got on the PA system and declared a school-wide investigation when that came out. The *Barker* makes a difference!

Sometimes Avalon pushes it too far, like when she demanded the resignation of whichever PTA member chose Flaxplosion bars for the big fundraiser. That was a little close to home. A lot of kids know that my mother is the guilty party—including Kevin, who also works on the *Barker* staff. He had a lot to say on the subject. Kevin has a lot to say about everything.

Avalon became a legend at the *Barker* two years ago, when she was only in sixth grade. She came up with the idea for the annual Brightling Teacher of the Year contest. Basically, we put out a box in the hall outside the *Barker* office and kids can come and vote for their favorite teacher. When we release the results, it's always the *Barker*'s most popular issue. Avalon says we have to print triple the usual number of copies that week, and our webpage gets a lot more views too.

I'm at one of the iPads, working on my latest feature—"THE BOBCATS' WINNING STREAK: AN INSIDER'S VIEW"—when Avalon finishes counting the day's votes.

"Who is this Aidact guy?" she asks. "I've never heard of him."

"He's new," Kevin supplies from the desk where he works on his weekly column, Krumlich's Korner. "He teaches mostly seventh-grade classes."

"And he's coach of the Bobcats," I add. "The team really likes him."

It leaves kind of a sour taste in my mouth, because so does my mother. But you can't deny the results. The Bobcats are *winning*. And it's more than just great coaching. It's that Mr. Aidact supports us one million percent. In games, he fights every bad call that goes against us and he's never wrong. It's almost like he has slow-motion video replay running nonstop in his head, so he can see what nobody else can. When you get whistled for a foul that's not your fault, he's right there in the umpire's face. Around the league, the officials have started calling him Eagle Eyes. When you've got someone like that on your side, you feel like nothing can stop you.

"Well, Aidact just moved into first place," Avalon informs us. "He got twenty-seven new votes today. That's more than Miss Muro."

I'm impressed. Miss Muro teaches Film History, the most popular class in the whole school. It's at eight thirty a.m. and all they do is turn out the lights and watch movies. So it's like getting an extra forty-five minutes of sleep. She wins every year.

"I voted for Mr. Zelcer," Kevin announces in his usual superior tone. "He's the best teacher for advanced students. Mr. Aidact has been on a slide ever since he started holding Trivia Club in detention."

Big talk from a guy whose whole life is pretty trivial.

Avalon's thoughtful. "A brand-new teacher winning the contest. There could be a real story here. Newbie makes good—I like the sound of that."

"I'll write about it in Krumlich's Korner," Kevin offers.

"Well . . ." Avalon hesitates. She knows that nobody reads Krumlich's Korner, not even Kevin's mother, I'll bet. A dedicated journalist like Avalon is probably itching to fire Kevin, except there's no firing in middle school. "Maybe Rosalie should take this assignment. She's on the field hockey team, so she's got more than the student perspective. She's got the player perspective too."

159

I'm a little torn. On the one hand, it feels great that an A-list eighth grader like Avalon has faith in me as a reporter. And Kevin looks ticked off, which is just gravy. On the other hand, I picture Mr. Aidact's intense blue eyes gazing off the front page of the *Barker*. When Mom sees that—and my byline on the article—she might try to invite him over for dinner or something. Mr. Aidact is a great coach and a good teacher, but I don't want him as my stepdad. I already have a father, thank you very much.

"What do you say, Rosalie?" Avalon prompts. "I think you could really knock this one out of the park."

"Don't you mean score on a penalty corner?" I joke.

She looks at me like I've lost my marbles. Everybody pretends to care about field hockey when the team is on a winning streak, but nobody knows anything about it.

That's okay. I'm on a special assignment from Avalon Pappas. If I nail this, next year's editor in chief could be me!

✳

I was planning on asking Mr. Aidact for an interview, but then I get a better idea. I call it "A Day in the Life of a Rising Star." I don't spy on him exactly. I just try to be a fly on the wall so I can get a sense of the real him and why he's becoming so popular among the students.

8:05 a.m. Mr. Aidact's first stop in the morning is the playing field, where he spreads sawdust over any puddles or wet spots from last night's rain. That way, by the time practice rolls around, the field will be dry. Mr. Perkins is with him, but he just watches.

8:25 a.m. Stinky Newhouse is already waiting for Mr. Aidact outside room 233. They exchange high fives and fist bumps and go into some kind of back-and-forth rap battle. Come to think of it, I seem to remember that a lot of the votes I saw yesterday looked suspiciously like Stinky's notorious chicken-scratch handwriting.

9:50 a.m. En route to second period, Booker Capshaw drops his model of a magnesium sulfate heptahydrate molecule down the back stairs, sending multicolored balls, springs, and connectors scattering in all directions. While Booker groans about three weeks' work down the drain, Mr. Aidact organizes a team to bring him the pieces. His hands just a blur, he reassembles the molecule in about thirty seconds. Miracle number one of the day. When he's finished, the kids in the stairwell give him a standing ovation.

10:15 a.m. Mia Spinelli shows up an hour and forty-five minutes late for school. When Mr. Aidact gives her a detention, she puts her hand on her heart, like it's a great honor.

11:35 a.m. The cafeteria. Mr. Aidact breaks up a food fight by making an incredible bare-handed catch of a flying grapefruit that could have taken somebody's head off. Then, with the entire lunchroom watching, he fires the grapefruit with deadly accuracy into the trash can sixty feet away.

He never even takes time to eat lunch himself. He moves from table to table, chatting with everybody. There isn't a single topic of conversation he can't join into—from Harley-Davidson motorcycles to designer tracksuits to *The Lord of the Rings*. It's like he knows *everything*.

12:20 p.m. As Mr. Aidact finishes lunch duty, I spy my mother through the glass doors, hurrying down the main hall. Oh no—the last thing I need is for Mom to see him and barge into the cafeteria on a flirting mission. Thinking on my feet, I grab a leftover hard-boiled egg, smash it into the center of my forehead, and wail for the teacher on duty. Mr. Aidact brings me into the kitchen to get cleaned up, and by the time we're done, the coast is clear. It isn't great journalism to become a part of your own story, and Avalon would never approve. But she doesn't have to know. And I learn another important fact about Mr. Aidact. He's really nice—even to someone weird enough to egg her own face.

1:05 p.m. The building thermostat goes haywire, and suddenly the temperature in all the rooms is eighty-eight degrees and rising. Sweat pours off everybody—students and teachers alike. Kids are slipping in perspiration puddles in the hall. We're too sluggish and uncomfortable to get any work done. But that's okay—none of the teachers can hold it together to assign anything. All except Mr. Aidact. He's fresh as a daisy. His step is as energetic as ever. No droplets running down his face, no sweat stains on his clothes. Mr. Perkins can't even muster the strength to lug his briefcase from room to room. Mr. Aidact has to carry it for him. Pretty soon he might have to carry Mr. Perkins.

3:30 p.m. The heating guys fixed the problem, so the temperature in the school is back to normal. Field hockey practice starts in half an hour, but Mr. Aidact's teaching responsibilities aren't over yet. The crowd outside the detention room boils halfway down the hall to the library, and the air crackles with excitement. Song lyrics roll off tongues and kids quiz one another at trivia, preparing to go up against the master. Through the chatter, one name rises above the general buzz: Aidact.

"If you play *Jeopardy!* against Mr. Aidact, you're gonna get your butt whooped. . . ."

"He sank that grapefruit from a mile away. . . ."

"You can't stump Mr. Aidact. He knows old-school classic rock too. . . ."

"When the school got hot, I was afraid they might cancel detention. . . ."

"Any fool can build a carbon atom! This was magnesium sulfate heptahydrate. . . ."

I look around the sea of faces—not just regulars like Stinky, Mia, Oliver, and Nathan. I see straight-A students, jocks, Model UN kids, science fair stars, and even fellow reporters from the *Barker*. There's no way everybody here has detention today. There aren't this many troublemakers in San Quentin, much less one middle school.

These people aren't all in detention; they're coming to detention because detention is the place to be. And there's only one reason for that.

Somehow, Mr. Aidact has turned *punishment* into an after-school event that people are lining up to get into. If that doesn't make him Brightling Teacher of the Year, I don't know what does.

✳

It isn't official until the voting closes. One morning, Avalon brings in the ballot box and plops it on her editor's desk.

"Well, it's a landslide. Mr. Aidact won by a hundred and twenty-seven votes. That's the biggest margin ever."

I'm not surprised at all. In fact, I was so sure Mr. Aidact would win that I wrote up my article last night so I could give it to Avalon the minute the results came in.

As I hand her the pages, I'm especially proud of the headline, in thirty-point block capitals: "A STAR IS BORN."

CONFIDENTIAL REPORT

To: Department of Education, Washington, DC
From: Paul Perkins, PE
Project: AIDACT

A troubling trend is emerging that the Department did not anticipate. Since AIDACT is constantly surrounded by middle schoolers, many of the behaviors learned by the AI system are adolescent in nature. While AIDACT, obviously, cannot experience fun, the AI constantly trains itself to classify some activities as more desirable than others. This creates a feedback loop of adolescent thinking, resulting in conduct that can only be described as immature.

I performed adjustments on AIDACT's right hand to repair minor damage incurred during numerous high fives. Fist bumps are also a concern. Further study required.

PROJECT STATUS: Yellow

SPECIAL EXPENSES
Dry cleaning (see supplemental report: "Food Fight")

Paul Perkins, PE

The *PE* stands for professional engineer. It's an extra certification; not all engineers have it. It means I know how things work because I'm the one who makes them work.

I never expected to be an employee of the Department of Education, but the AIDACT Project was irresistible. Artificial intelligence is the future, and here was a chance to be on the cutting edge.

My specialties are computers, cybernetics, and robotics. What I'm not good at is dealing with middle school kids, with their bad attitudes, their raging hormones, and their loud and rebellious disrespect.

I'm not complaining about the students, by the way. To be honest, I barely notice them. They aren't my responsibility at all. I'm not a real student teacher—that's just a ruse to explain my presence in the building alongside the AIDACT unit as it grows into the teaching job it was designed for.

No, my complaint is with "Mr. Aidact" himself, who is turning into a petulant, self-centered adolescent just like the students around him. There's no problem with his artificial intelligence. On the contrary, the AI system is working *too* well. He's picking up every single bad habit from more than eight hundred kids, who spend all their time sharpening their bad habits to the level of high art. The unit isn't teaching them. He's *becoming* them.

Case in point: We're in the apartment, preparing for the nightly software diagnostic, and I can't help noticing that the unit seems a little shorter than before. Obviously, this is impossible. An AIDACT unit is constructed of polymers, metals, and circuitry; it can't shrink or grow. So I perform a visual inspection. The shoulders are hunched slightly forward, one hip is higher than the other, and the opposite knee is bent. He's *slouching*—just like most of Brightling Middle School!

"Correct your posture," I tell him.

"Make me," comes the reply.

I almost snap back that, as project engineer, I *can* make him. But then I realize it's not true. The way an AIDACT unit is designed, the AI system has much more influence on behavior than anything I could do. I have the ability to shut him down, but I can't give him an attitude adjustment, which is what he really needs.

You'll notice I've started calling the unit "he" rather than "it." This isn't Department of Education policy. It just happened. It's not unusual with AI, in situations where machines take on human qualities: *It* is acting in a way that is unexpected. *He* is getting on my nerves.

When I open up the back panel to reveal the main USB port, the unit heaves an exasperated sigh. Again, a robot is incapable of exasperation. But an AI system can re-create it as taught by eight hundred experts.

"What's the problem?" I ask.

"I hate these software diagnostics," he complains.

That's another thing about middle school. Preface anything with "I hate" and you'll fit right in.

"It's necessary," I remind him.

"It's boring."

"You are not capable of boredom," I remind him with just a touch of impatience.

"You can't make me do this. It's not fair."

169

"Want to bet?" I snap. I'm not proud of that. Engineers do not get angry at machines.

I feel like Geppetto, watching Pinocchio turn into a real boy. But the lonely wood-carver had it easy.

Pinocchio never went to middle school.

✳

It's one thing to be saddled with a typical teenager in the form of a $250 million government project. That's just annoying. But when it begins to affect the AIDACT unit's performance as a teacher, it becomes a major cause of concern.

The good news is the unit hasn't lost the ability to follow a lesson plan, teach a class, and respond to student questions, accessing the entirety of human knowledge via the internet. The problem is that his role at the school has grown so vast—from staff member to athletic coach to bus supervisor to quizmaster to lunchroom monitor to sympathetic ear to cruise director of detention—that he's too easily distracted.

Don't get me wrong—he's certainly *popular*. The kids *love* him. The school newspaper, the Brightling *Barker*, just named him Teacher of the Year. I'm sure that's never happened to a robot before. Mr. Aidact has *fans*. There's that Steinke character, whose lone ambition is to come up with a song lyric his beloved teacher won't recognize—something that could only happen during a massive internet outage. No pastime exists, no fandom, no hobby, no interest that Mr. Aidact can't instantly become an expert in. He knows more sports statistics than Darryl Yarmolenko and more trivia than Kevin Krumlich. He can take on the entire chess club at once and beat them all in less than fifteen moves. Thanks to the advanced circuitry in his nimble fingers, he's equally adept with a video game controller or a pair of knitting needles. He can play the piano, or carry it up a flight of stairs, if necessary. He has endless patience for the ongoing soap opera that is Mia Spinelli. Mia told me he's the only adult who listens to her ". . . because he's so *human*."

Guess what, Mia: he's the only adult who *isn't*. And by the way, he's isn't even an adult. He was assembled nine months ago.

The other teachers at Brightling were very quick to jump on the AIDACT bandwagon when they realized they could dump their unwanted duties and assignments onto him. For them, it was like Christmas and the Fourth of July all wrapped up in one. No more bus duty or lunch duty or recess duty. No more long afternoons covering detention. A few of them even have Mr. Aidact grading papers for them. The optical technology in the unit's eyes is capable of processing two million multiple-choice answers per second—although physically handling the test papers is a lot slower than that.

I spoke up against it and was outvoted, fifty to one. The argument was always "He doesn't mind."

"Of course he doesn't," I agree. "A machine is incapable of *minding* anything. My objection is based on the fact that this isn't part of the AIDACT project. You are using government property for nongovernment purposes!"

"Property." Lee Benrahma makes a face. "That's such a harsh word to describe a nice guy like Rob Aidact."

He means a "nice guy" who's willing to set out orange traffic cones during a sleet storm while the custodians hide in the faculty lounge drinking coffee.

Well, all that's in the past. Now that Mr. Aidact is so popular, the staff is turning against him. It's the Teacher of the Year thing that's put it over the top. No one wants to lose a popularity contest to a machine.

"If I have to read one more essay about how he's the person they admire most, I'm going to scream," Syesha Berg announces as we sit down to lunch one day. "Not Shakespeare or Albert Einstein or even Taylor Swift."

I'd pay money to hear Syesha scream. I'm sure it comes out in the same monotone she uses for everything else.

Kelly Tapper shoots me a resentful look. "*He* gets to be the fun teacher with his song lyrics and his trivia quizzes and his winning sports team. And who assigns homework and calls parents and gives failing grades? That's us. No wonder we're not Teacher of the Year."

I clear my throat carefully. "Can I just ask you to remember what you're getting mad at? A robot."

From the other side of the door, in the main cafeteria, we hear a roar of approval from hundreds of throats, followed by a round of applause.

"It's him, isn't it?" Tina Muro—last year's Teacher of the Year—says in a mournful tone. "He's caught another grapefruit or swallowed a whole lasagna or balanced a tray on his head."

"He doesn't eat," I remind her gently, "so the lasagna's out."

I should technically be with my AIDACT. I'm not supposed to let the unit out of my sight. He used to come in here with me while I had lunch, but he refuses now. The faculty lounge is full of "stiffs." They're too boring. He prefers to be out there with the kids. No wonder they like him so much.

AIDACT's greatest fans are his field hockey girls. Every single one of them is absolutely convinced that it's his coaching that has led them to victory after victory after victory. I can't even disagree with that. The AI system is programmed in such a way that it would teach itself coaching the same way it would teach itself anything else. Plus, it picks up on the team's emotions, so he argues every call, cheers every defensive play, and celebrates every goal right along with them. To the girls, it sends the message that he's one of them. And it doesn't hurt that he has instant access to every millisecond of video and every word about field hockey ever posted to the web. At first, that's just a dump of data. But as he's exposed to more game situations, his AI will get better and better at understanding how to use all that information. Who am I to say that he isn't an effective coach?

Since I'm in charge of the unit, I've been right there for every second of this roller-coaster ride. The players call me the assistant coach, although nothing could be further from the truth. Even if I were a die-hard sports fan—and I'm not—field hockey wouldn't be very high on my list. The stick is like a J—a club with a tiny hook at the end. It's a miracle to me that anyone can move a ball with it. And I'll bet the rulebook is longer and more complicated than all the computer code in an AID-ACT's AI system. The whistle sounds *constantly* because two sticks touched, or somebody kicked the ball or hit the ball with the wrong part of the stick. Kudos to the girls for making sense of any of it. I never will.

When the closing whistle signifies the Bobcats' seventh straight win, my AIDACT unit is right at the center of the seething, bouncing, triumphant players. In fact, he's leaping higher than any of the girls and I consider making a note on his ankle and knee construction. Perhaps both could use a little extra reinforcement.

Onto the scene charge a few of our fans—friends, siblings, parents. In the lead is the PTA president—Rosalie Arnette's mother. She hits the circle of celebration, plows her way in, and throws her arms around Mr. Aidact. I didn't work for the Department of Education when the AIDACT model was first designed, but I'll bet this is something nobody anticipated. The faculty knows exactly what Mr. Aidact is and what he isn't, but that information was never extended to the community. So now we have a real human parent who seems to be sweet on our robot.

This is a bigger problem than it may appear to be. I can't tell her about Mr. Aidact without compromising the secrecy of the project. How could I be sure that she wouldn't then spread the word to the entire town?

I sneak closer, in an effort to eavesdrop on their conversation. It's hard to hear much in the general din, but I distinctly pick up her words: ". . . go out to celebrate."

My mind races. It's impossible to predict how an AIDACT unit will respond to an invitation like that. It certainly isn't part of the original programming. But we've learned over the past weeks that the AI system sometimes takes Mr. Aidact in unexpected directions.

I don't catch his answer because at that moment, Leticia's little brother knocks my tool case off the bench. As it hits the ground, the clasp pops open, spilling the contents all over the grass. In a heartbeat, I'm on my hands and knees, restoring expensive and delicate instruments to their proper places.

"Hey, these are cool!"

The young boy reaches for a digital calibrator, and I have to hold myself back from slapping his hand away. The kid paws everything he can get his grubby little hands on, asking, "What does this do?" and "Why is this so shiny?" and "Can I keep this one?"

"No!" I snap.

"But you have so many!"

I'm finally able to snap the case shut and get back to my feet. That's when I notice that Mr. Aidact is no longer at the center of the group of victorious field hockey players. They're still celebrating—except for Rosalie, who's looking in consternation across the field. I follow her gaze to the parking lot, where I see something no supervising engineer should ever be forced to see: my AIDACT unit getting into a black BMW with Mrs. Arnette.

"Hey! Come back!" I take off after them, the heavy case battering my knees as I run. I have no idea what I'm going to say if I catch up to them. I can't reveal that Mr. Aidact is a robot, but at the same time, I'm not supposed to let him out of my sight. I can demand to go on their "date" with them, but that won't make any sense either. I'm supposed to be his student teacher, not his nanny!

Fate makes the decision for me. Just as I pass through the gate, the BMW takes a left out of the lot and starts away down the street. Sprinting now, I run to my car so I can follow them. But as I steer into my own turn onto the main road, I realize there's no one to follow. They're out of sight.

Reality descends on me like a heavy curtain. I've just lost $250 million worth of government property.

I weigh my options. I can send a wireless command to return at once, but there's no guarantee that the unit will obey it. The AI system has the final say over AID-ACT's actions. That was an essential part of the project. The Department of Education has to know that it can fully trust the unit to make good decisions on behalf of students. Nowadays, with AIDACT acting like a defiant middle schooler, it's almost a sure thing that any message from me will be ignored.

Besides, there's one more way to find him. The unit is equipped with a GPS tracking chip. My hands trembling, I pull over to the curb, take out my phone, and tap the app. A town map appears, with a blinking light moving slowly along the road about a mile ahead of my current position. I take a deep breath and try to calm the rapid-fire beating of my heart. I've got him.

I'm so focused on my phone screen that I almost rear-end a garbage truck as I speed along, hoping to catch up to the BMW. Yikes! I slam on the brakes and endure some angry honking from behind. I force it out of my mind. Finding the unit has to be my only priority.

The blinking tracker seems to have stopped. At the last second, I spot the BMW pulling into the mini-mall to my right. I'm too late to make the turn, but luckily, there's a second entrance a few hundred yards ahead. By the time I pull onto the property and backtrack to the BMW, Rosalie's mother is leading the AIDACT unit up the outdoor staircase to a romantic-looking café called L'Auberge.

What is he thinking? The unit is incapable of eating or drinking. Sometimes artificial intelligence seems more like actual stupidity. At the same time, the system is programmed to mimic the behavior of people around him. It must be telling him to go along with this!

I have to put a stop to it—even if that means calling attention to a government secret.

I get out of the car and muster my strength to shout up to them. I have no idea what I'm planning to say. I only know that it has to be loud and it has to be *now*.

I'm just about to open my mouth when another voice—a younger one—calls, "Hey, it's Mr. Aidact!"

A group of Brightling kids stands at the entrance to a Dave & Buster's arcade, waving at their teacher at the top of the stairs. I pick out Steinke, Darryl, Mia, and a few other familiar faces.

Mr. Aidact appears at the top of the stairs. "Hi, pupils! What up?"

Mrs. Arnette bobs into view, and a second kid asks, "Is that your wife?"

"It's Peggy Arnette, PTA president," he reports, supplying the information exactly as it was originally given to him. "Arnette is her married name. She's recently divorced."

"You want to come to Dave and Buster's, Mr. Aidact?" a girl asks. "It'll be really fun!"

I notice the familiar head tilt that means the unit is accessing the internet. He must like what he learns about Dave & Buster's because a moment later, he comes rushing down the stairs to join the kids, leaving Mrs. Arnette staring after him, open-mouthed.

By the time I make it into the arcade, Mr. Aidact is seated at a video game called NASCAR, piloting a souped-up race car, while the kids cheer him on.

"Faster, Mr. Aidact!"

"Downshift!"

"Get out of the car! You're on fire!"

A miffed Mrs. Arnette shows up a few minutes later. "Oh, it's you," she says to me.

I feel bad for her, but obviously, I can't explain why her "date" was a bust.

"I guess he's a kid at heart," I offer as kindly as I can.

"Seriously, what's his deal?" she persists.

"He loves teaching," I reply. "You could almost say he was made for it."

Mr. Aidact exchanges high fives with his admirers, while on-screen, his character is draped in a victory wreath.

"It doesn't look much like teaching to me," she comments sourly.

"You don't have to stick around," I tell her. "I'll give him a ride home."

"Thanks." She doesn't seem very thankful, but she does leave. That's the main thing.

I walk her to the door. When I turn back, I find myself face-to-face with my AIDACT unit.

"I need money," he informs me.

"You got on that racing game just fine," I point out.

"Darryl paid for that with his card. I want my own card. Nobody likes a mooch."

When the Department of Education first proposed the $250 million AIDACT project, I'll bet not one penny was budgeted for a Dave & Buster's card because their robot wouldn't want to be a mooch.

Pretty soon my unit and his middle school friends are weighed down with miles of prize tickets. There is no game of skill an AIDACT can't master after a small amount of trial and error. A quarter of a billion dollars buys you not just an android classroom teacher but also a world champion Skee-Ball player. Dave & Buster's employees are beginning to look worried. If this keeps up, they'll be cleaned out of prizes by closing time. I'm worried too—not because of the prizes, but because how am I ever going to get him out of here, short of opening up his chest and shutting off power? He's having far too much of what his AI classifies as fun.

I start to get insistent. "We have to leave!" I urge.

"Five more minutes," he wheedles.

And I make the fatal mistake of turning my back.

The next thing I know, he's at the Test Your Strength booth, the big mallet raised up high over his head.

The kids chant a countdown. "Five . . . four . . . three . . . two . . . one . . ."

"No—" I gasp.

The mallet comes down with an earsplitting crack. The target shatters. The indicator shoots straight up, takes the bell clean off with a resounding clang, and keeps on going until it knocks out a spray of ceiling tiles. Sparks fly in all directions as the entire booth collapses in on itself.

Dave & Buster's decides to close early.

"Everybody brags about school spirit," Steinke explains, "but only *we* have a teacher who can shut down a Dave and Buster's."

"Yeah, Mr. Aidact!" Darryl adds reverently. "You don't know your own strength!"

He's right. Only I know the strength of a fully functional AIDACT unit. And I still wasn't able to prevent this from happening.

It's the first inkling I get that this project might be in serious trouble.

22

Oliver Zahn

One thing I never thought I'd get a chance to do: teach a teacher how to make spitballs.

Then again, I never expected to have a teacher like Mr. Aidact.

He sits at a cafeteria table opposite Nathan and me, and we can see his jaw working hard as he chews a piece of loose-leaf paper into a ball.

"Good," I say. "Now insert the projectile into this hollowed-out pen."

The teacher drops the spitball into his hand and tries to stuff it into the launcher. But it won't go. That's when

I notice it isn't a spitball at all; it's just a lump of crushed paper.

"It's dry," Nathan whispers in my ear. "He has no saliva."

I should have known. Mr. Aidact is an incredibly life-like robot, but machines don't have saliva, because they don't need it. And you can't make a spitball without spit.

"Here." I reach out my water bottle and dribble a few droplets onto the paper wad. "Now it should work better."

Mr. Aidact chews a little more and out comes a perfect round ball. The blue eyes look to me for approval.

I nod. "It's a thing of beauty. Now all you need is a target. Who could use a big wet smackeroo right in the back of the head?"

"Why would anybody want that?" he asks innocently.

"They wouldn't," I explain. "That's what makes it funny."

A big frown. "And it *isn't* funny if I shoot at someone who *does* want to be hit by it?"

Our teacher may have a computer brain, but as a class clown, he's a total loss.

In the end, he doesn't use the launcher. He's a robot teacher, not a leaf blower—no wind power. Instead, he flicks the projectile off his thumb with a snap of his forefinger. And what a snap! His first spitball slams into today's lunch menu, which is posted outside the food line. His second effort strikes a bull's-eye in the *r* in *Brightling* on our wall mural. With the last, he rattles the picture window that looks out over the athletic field. That's on the very far side of the cafeteria, close to a hundred feet away.

"Wow," Nathan breathes.

"Legit," Mr. Aidact comments. He sounds about as close to pleased with himself as a robot can get.

Nathan is nervous as we make our way to our lockers after lunch. "Good thing he didn't hit anybody! Did you see that last shot? It was a bullet!"

"Not bad for a newbie," I agree.

"Seems to me our teacher is a better rule-wrecker than you."

I snort. "What rule did he wreck? He could have dropped one of those spitballs into a bowl of soup. Or nailed his buddy Perkins right between the eyes. Or put one on the back of somebody's sweater so they'd carry it around all day like a Kick Me sign. Hundreds of kids in that cafeteria, and what does he target? Windows and walls. There are two parts to rule-wrecking. First, you need skills. Mr. Aidact has those—I give him props. But more important, you need a sense of humor to tell you how to use them."

Nathan reaches for his locker and starts twisting in the combination. "And no robot teacher is ever going to have one of those."

As the afternoon goes on, I start to pick up on a strange undercurrent of conversation in the school. Teachers' names are being randomly tossed around—something I definitely frown on. Kids shouldn't waste too much time thinking about teachers, unless you're deciding whose chair to superglue.

And these aren't just *conversations* about teachers. It's almost like there's a gigantic game of Clue going on and the whole school is trying to identify the "killer"—like Mr. Zelcer in the conservatory with the lead pipe.

"I think it's Mr. Tomlinson," I overhear Ainsley saying in social studies.

"It's Miss Tapper," Laki tells her. "I saw her with a can of motor oil out in the parking lot this morning."

Ainsley shrugs. "Maybe she needed it for her car."

They get pretty heated discussing it. I mean, who takes their motor oil that seriously?

I bring up the subject with Nathan during class change. "Is it just me, or are people obsessing on teachers today?"

"Something's up," he confirms with his usual worried expression. "I just saw Booker and Rosalie going over a copy of the yearbook. It was open to the staff page, and they were circling faces and putting Xs through others."

"Did they say why?"

He shrugs. "I didn't get a chance to ask them. They took off as soon as the bell rang."

Class after class, it goes on—mini arguments about who "it" could be. Teachers' names tossed in the air like juggling pins. Suspects ruled out for reasons that don't make any sense.

"It can't be Miss Muro. She had a nosebleed on Monday—and it was real blood."

Why would anybody expect Miss Muro to bleed *fake* blood?

"Mrs. Aguilar had a baby last year. . . ."

"I saw Coach Gilderoy sneeze once. . . ."

"This is too weird," Nathan complains. "*Everybody* sneezes! Seems to me there isn't one teacher in this whole school who's never . . ." His voice trails off.

Both of us realize it at the same instant. There *is* one teacher at our school who doesn't sneeze. Or bleed.

Sneezing, bleeding, having babies—these are all things that humans do and robots don't.

Nathan is horrified. "They found out about Mr. Aidact?"

I shake my head. "Then they wouldn't be guessing about Coach Gilderoy or Miss Muro. This is more like somebody started a rumor that there's a robot teacher at our school."

"But we're the only ones who know that!"

It plays in my mind like an old movie, with jumpy action and scratchy sound: The two of us standing by our lockers. Nathan's words: ". . . And no robot teacher is ever going to have one of those."

It hits me—Kevin Krumlich's locker is right around the corner from ours.

"Krumlich!" I rasp in true pain. "He must have overheard us! And he blabbed to the whole school!"

"This is bad," Nathan moans. "Project AIDACT comes from the Department of Education. If it falls apart it'll be *our fault*!"

"Maybe no one will figure out who the real robot is," I offer hopefully. "The kids in this town aren't exactly geniuses. I know a bunch of high schoolers who can't tell the difference between a bag of candy and a broken trophy wrapped in a Batman cape."

Poor Nathan. He doesn't have the mental toughness of a true rule-wrecker. He's panicking. "We're going to get kicked out of school and you're making jokes!"

"You know what we need?" I decide. "A red herring."

"How can you talk about fish at a time like this?"

"A red herring is a fake clue to distract people," I explain. "Like if we don't want kids to find out about Mr. Aidact, we've got to give them another robot teacher to sink their teeth into."

"What do you mean, 'another robot teacher'?"

"How about Mrs. Berg?" I suggest, brainstorming rapidly. "I don't think she's changed expression since we started here in sixth grade. And that voice! It would put a Tasmanian Devil to sleep."

"Yeah, but—"

"Syesha Berg," I muse. "Sy Berg. *Cyborg*. Now, that's what I call a robot."

Nathan looks like his head is spinning. You'd think he'd be used to me, but no. When the ideas really start rolling, it can be hard for him to keep up.

"So what happens now?" he asks in a small voice. "How do we spread it around the school that Mrs. Berg is the robot?"

I beam at him. "Same way. We just have to let it slip in front of Krumlich. That's as good as a front page ad in the *New York Times*."

23

Nathan Popova

I feel guilty every time I see Mrs. Berg.

Guilt plus an Oliver Alert is a killer combination. The only reason I went along with the whole red herring thing was I couldn't think of another way to protect Mr. Aidact's identity. So we let our Sy Berg/Cyborg "theory" slip in front of Kevin. He took care of the rest, spreading the story like pink eye. There may be a couple of white mice in the science lab who haven't heard yet. Everybody else knows.

Half the time, I follow Oliver because I haven't got my own plan. And later, when we're both getting chewed out in the principal's office, a dozen better ideas come to me. But by then it's too late.

"You've got nothing to feel guilty about," Oliver challenges me. "Kids used to sleep while Berg droned on in class. Now they hang on her every word."

"Yeah—because they're afraid she'll blow a transformer and burn down the school."

We watch as Mrs. Berg is escorted onto the bus by a few kids from her homeroom. One of them carries her purse. Another helps her up to the bottom step like she's made out of delicate crystal.

"She's never had it so good," Oliver insists. "If the *Barker* held another Teacher of the Year vote, she'd win by a mile. Robots are box office gold."

"Except she *isn't* one." The alert is tolling in my ears. "Mr. Aidact is."

He shrugs. "The truth is overrated."

Speaking of Mr. Aidact, he's at the front of the bus, ushering our class aboard along with Mrs. Berg's group. Our two homerooms are going on a field trip to the Hickenlooper Outdoor Center, about thirty miles from town. It's a seventh-grade tradition at Brightling. We go orienteering. The way Mr. Aidact described it, they take you out to the middle of nowhere and lose you. And you have to find your way back to the Hickenlooper Center, using a compass and a series of directions. It's a combination of PE, science, geography, and problem solving.

"And medieval torture," I add as I take my seat on the bus beside Oliver. I'm not the outdoorsy type.

"Stick with me, you guys," Kevin calls from across the aisle. "I won't let you get lost."

"I'm sticking with Mrs. Berg." Oliver drops his voice to a whisper. "See how one earlobe is a little longer than the other? Built-in GPS."

"Shhh!" Kevin warns. "No one's supposed to know about that."

Big talk from the kid who's the reason *everyone* knows about that.

"There's nothing to worry about," Rosalie bursts in from a couple of rows behind. "The PTA sponsors this trip every year, and no one's ever disappeared."

"We'll mark our trail with Flaxplosion bars," Oliver offers. "Not even the squirrels will touch them. They'll be around till the next Ice Age."

"If nobody ever disappears, how come Mrs. Berg is on her feet every two minutes, doing a head count?" I mumble to Oliver as we merge onto the freeway.

"Not very robot-like," he replies disapprovingly. "Mr. Aidact didn't count us even once. He *knows* how many 'pupils' he's supposed to come back with."

When we get to the Hickenlooper Center, most of the kids want to skip the orienteering and go straight to the gift shop. That sounds like a pretty good idea to me because it's starting to drizzle outside. Kevin is trying to convince Mrs. Berg not to leave the building, but he refuses to give her a reason why not. I think he believes that if she gets too wet, she'll short-circuit or rust or something. That makes no sense because Mr. Aidact is always holding field hockey practice in the rain, and nothing bad ever happens to him. Those panels on his body must be waterproof.

Perkins refuses to leave his briefcase on the bus, no matter how many times the Hickenlooper people tell him he can't bring it out on the trails. But he also refuses to stay at the welcome center, since he never lets Mr. Aidact out of his sight.

It seems like a standoff until the student teacher shows the head ranger an ID inside his wallet. After that, it's all good and he's allowed to take his briefcase wherever he wants.

The rangers divide us up and give each group a compass and a sheet of directions. Oliver and I get paired with Rosalie and Kevin. Kevin, the big orienteer, puts himself in charge. Mistake number one. We're lost in the woods inside five minutes.

"Can't you even follow a simple series of directions?" Rosalie demands.

"I did!" Kevin defends himself. "Sort of."

"What's that supposed to mean?" I snap.

He buries his face in the instruction sheet, which is starting to look a little soggy. "We should have gone seventy-five paces at thirty-six degrees. I think we went thirty-six paces at seventy-five degrees. So we just have to backtrack and do it the right way."

But our backtracking can't be the right backtracking because it takes us to a giant squat tree with branches blocking the path—and we've definitely never been here before. That's when Kevin admits another problem—that we completed steps four and five before we did three. And when we try to bushwhack through the underbrush to where three might have brought us, we end up on the banks of a rushing stream, with no way to get across.

Kevin stares in consternation at the sheet. "You'd think they'd lead us to a bridge or at least stepping-stones."

"We're in the wrong place!" Rosalie explodes. "Because of *you*!"

At this point, Oliver is laughing until tears are running down his cheeks. Or maybe it's the rain, which is falling harder now.

"Yeah, sure, yuk it up," I tell him. "Seems to me we're going to die like dogs out here."

"Relax," he retorts. "We're not going to die. We've got phones. We can get rescued any time we want."

"Don't say 'rescued,'" Kevin snorts. "That sounds like we need help."

"What would you call what we need?" Rosalie asks savagely. "We're totally lost, thanks to you!"

"No, we're not," Kevin insists. "All we have to do is follow *these*." As he brandishes our printed directions, a gust of wind tears the page from his hand and sends it fluttering into the water. In a matter of seconds, the current takes it far downstream.

"*Now* we need help," Oliver cackles.

"Our directions!" I exclaim. I've been so obsessed with my Oliver Alerts that I never thought to put in a Krumlich Alarm.

"They were useless anyway," Rosalie says mournfully. "How could we follow them? We're too turned around to know where we started from."

We decide that our best bet is to walk along the water until we come to a bridge or a narrow spot where we can cross over. We've been at this about twenty minutes, sliding through deepening mud until our sneakers look like chocolate-covered rocks, when we come upon another group on the opposite side of the stream.

"You guys got lost too, huh?" I call to Ainsley.

"Are you kidding? We're killing it!" She waves her instruction sheet. "According to this, the welcome center should be just two hundred paces beyond that rise." She seems happy, almost perky. Her group members are full of energy and smiles, exchanging jokes and high fives. She indicates the trail, which leads up and over a steep hill. It's easy to believe the Hickenlooper Center is right there. Frankly, I don't care if the Emerald City is right there. It doesn't help us. We're on *the wrong side of the river*!

Ainsley seems to notice this for the first time. "Hey, how did you guys get over there?"

"Ask Krumlich," Oliver offers. "He's our leader."

Her group-mates are starting up the slope. "Come on, Ainsley," Laki calls. "They've got free hot chocolate at the welcome center!"

"Do you guys want me to tell Mr. Aidact you're stuck?" she asks us.

"Of course not." Kevin laughs it off. "We know exactly what we're doing."

I'm not sure how I keep myself from planting my foot dead center between his butt cheeks, but it's a show of restraint I'm proud of.

"Why would you say that?" Rosalie raves once Ainsley has disappeared into the trees of the opposite hill.

"We are never going to find our way to the other side! For all we know, the next bridge is miles downstream! We're cold! We're wet! We're filthy! *And they have hot chocolate!*"

"I say we throw Kevin in the water and use *him* as a bridge," Oliver suggests.

We're in a real dilemma. We could continue our search for a place to cross. But if Ainsley's right, that would only take us farther away from the welcome center. As we stand there, debating our options, the rain turns into a full downpour. Pretty soon you can barely see the top of the hill as the storm settles low over us.

Oliver takes out his phone. "I'm calling."

I stare at him. "Do you even have Mr. Aidact's number?"

"I'll call the school. Someone will get in touch with him for us."

Before he can dial, we catch a flurry of motion starting down from the top of the hill. "*Pupils!*" calls a booming voice. "Stay where you are! I'm coming!"

Through the trees, we can make out the stalwart form of Mr. Aidact, hurrying down the path with a quick, sure-footed gait. Far behind him is a second figure, lurching in fits and starts, descending one step and slipping another two. It's Perkins, struggling along awkwardly, unbalanced by his bulky briefcase.

"We're saved!" Rosalie cheers.

"No, we're not," I point out. "There's still the river, you know."

"We don't need saving," Kevin insists. "Everything's under control."

A big gap opens between the two teachers as Mr. Aidact marches purposefully out of the trees toward us. I check for an expression of worry or grim determination on his face, but he looks like he always looks—pleasant, relaxed, friendly.

He strides up to the water's edge *and plows right into the rushing stream*!

I don't know what I was expecting him to do, but it wasn't that.

A gasp escapes Rosalie. "Mr. Aidact—careful!"

Soon the water is up to his knees, then his hips. The current pulls at him, trying to drag him down, but he doesn't even notice it. Then he's standing in front of us, dripping muddy water from the waist down.

"It's not my fault!" Kevin tells him. "These guys got me lost!"

Mr. Aidact grabs Rosalie with one arm and me with the other, lifting us up so our feet dangle off the ground. Without a word, he turns around and splashes back through the river, depositing us on the opposite bank. Then he crosses again and does the same thing with Kevin and Oliver. At last, the five of us are on the right side of the stream, panting with exertion—except Mr. Aidact. Robots don't pant.

"No-o-o!" Perkins is still working his way down the hill, but he speeds up at the sight of Mr. Aidact carrying us across the water. "You *can't*—I mean you *shouldn't*—"

"My pupils needed me," Mr. Aidact replies.

"But the Department of Education—" Just as he's emerging from the trees, his swinging briefcase smacks against the last trunk, flips up, and strikes him dead center in the forehead. He drops like a stone and tumbles down the steep, muddy slope, landing with a splash in the stream. For a second, his pointy nose and glasses are above the rushing water, before the current closes over his face.

"He'll drown!" Rosalie shrills.

But Mr. Aidact is already on the move. He wades back into the river and drags Mr. Perkins ashore. The engineer is completely drenched. Blood oozes from the spot on his forehead where the corner of the briefcase clobbered him. Speaking of the case, he's still got it. His fingers are clamped onto the handle in a permanent grip.

His eyelids flutter, and he looks up at Mr. Aidact

and complains, "So cold . . ." before his eyes close again.

Mr. Aidact doesn't mess around. He throws Perkins's limp body over his shoulder like it's a sack of potatoes and starts up the hill. "Pupils—follow me!"

Which we do. We're too shocked not to. It was pretty lousy to be lost, soaked, and stuck on the wrong side of the river. But Mr. Perkins is really hurt. Even unconscious and half-drowned, he's still got an iron grip on the briefcase. Mr. Aidact pries it away from him and hands it to me. "Look after this. It's very important."

I feel like I'm being deputized by Superman himself. Mr. Aidact is a pretty big hero in my eyes right now. But the case weighs a ton, so it takes a lot to drag it up the slope. Oliver and I switch off, and between us, we manage to make it. When the welcome center appears over the rise, it's a beautiful sight.

The atrium is packed with kids from a few different tours, mingling, chattering, and sipping hot chocolate. That all comes to a sudden stop with Mr. Aidact's foghorn announcement: *"All Brightling pupils to the bus now! This is a legit emergency!"*

If it needs further explanation, the sight of the unconscious Perkins draped over the teacher's shoulder pretty much says it all.

It brings out the closest thing to a lively reaction

anyone has ever seen from Mrs. Berg. "What's going on?" she asks, taking in our soaked and bedraggled state. "What happened?"

"The directions were wrong," Kevin explains. "It wasn't my fault."

"I mean what happened to *him*?"

"He got taken out by his own briefcase," Oliver supplies.

Still lugging his student teacher, Mr. Aidact races out the door and across the parking lot. The two classes follow—there's something about carrying an unconscious guy that gives a person extra authority. When we board the bus, we find Perkins stretched out across a double seat at the front, still out cold. Oliver and I cram the briefcase into the leg space in front of him.

The student teacher causes a pretty big sensation among the kids as they pile on, while Mrs. Berg tries desperately to perform another head count in order to make sure nobody gets left behind. Kevin is telling everybody the story of what happened to the student teacher. Only in his version, *he* was the hero who rescued Perkins from "the raging rapids."

"That's everybody," Mrs. Berg confirms finally.

Mr. Aidact looks around. "Where's the bus driver?"

"He and a few other drivers went to a sandwich shop

in town," she replies. "I just called. They should be here in ten minutes."

In answer, Mr. Aidact sits down in the driver's seat and pulls the lever that shuts the door. "We don't have ten minutes." He turns the key and the engine roars to life.

"But"—Mrs. Berg drops her voice to a whisper—"You can't drive a bus! You're—*you*!"

Oliver stands up. "Yes, he can! He can do anything!"

Mr. Aidact tilts his head for several long seconds. At last he says, "I know everything there is to know about operating a motor vehicle."

It's a little jerky at first, and the bus stalls out a couple of times as Mr. Aidact gets the hang of shifting gears. Pretty soon, though, he's an expert, wheeling us onto the main highway back toward town. Oliver and I exchange a glance of understanding. We're the only kids who can picture Mr. Aidact's AI teaching itself to be an expert school bus driver, accessing maps and traffic laws from the internet.

Mrs. Berg is standing on the entrance steps, clutching the rail for dear life. "Where are we going?"

Another head tilt. "Mercy Hospital, four-forty-one Robinette Boulevard."

As Mr. Aidact becomes more comfortable behind the wheel, the bus picks up speed. A peek out the window confirms that the other cars are falling away behind us, and those in front are changing lanes to get out of our path. I breathe a silent prayer that we don't get pulled over for speeding. Considering he just taught himself how to drive eight minutes ago, I doubt he has a license. What are we supposed to do if our teacher gets arrested?

Mrs. Berg is thinking about that too. "Maybe we should slow down, Mr. Aidact." If this keeps up, no one is going to believe she's a robot anymore. There's nothing monotonous about her voice now.

Mr. Aidact steps harder on the gas. "Increased speed means an earlier time of arrival."

Normally, a bus ride is pretty loud, with everybody talking, laughing, arguing, and play fighting. Not this one. We're the quietest two classes in the history of school. It would be wrong to say you can hear a pin drop, but we can definitely hear the honking of other vehicles as Mr. Aidact cuts through traffic. We're all pretty relieved when we spot the blue-and-white H sign atop Mercy Hospital.

Mr. Aidact pilots the bus up to Emergency and screeches to a halt in a cloud of burning rubber. Then he scoops up Mr. Perkins like a bride and carries him in through the sliding doors. Fifty-four seventh graders are hot on his heels, Oliver and Rosalie in the lead.

Mrs. Berg tries to block the exit and keep us on the bus, but the crowd pushes right on past her.

"Stay where you are!" she orders. "I can't count you all!"

But even with the extra passion she's found today, her voice doesn't have the power and authority to shut down two classes on a mission.

We burst into Emergency, and the waiting room is instantly overwhelmed. Three nurses and a security guard rush to hold us back, and for a second, I wonder if we might plow right over them.

"That's our teacher!"

"And our student teacher!"

"It's an orienteering injury!"

"He got hit by a flying briefcase!"

"It's not my fault the directions were wrong!"

The last thing I see before we all get kicked out by security is Mr. Perkins being loaded onto a gurney by hospital staff. Then he and Mr. Aidact disappear behind the heavy doors.

Rosalie Arnette

I'm not sure exactly how I get past the waiting room and into the real hospital. One minute, I'm standing there with Oliver, and the next I'm backing up to let a wheelchair go by. I feel a rush of air as the heavy doors close behind me, and suddenly, I'm in and everybody else is out.

I'm super aware that I don't belong here in my soaked orienteering clothes, tracking mud from the knees down. But the place is so busy that nobody notices me. Doctors and nurses rush by; their eyes linger on me for a second or two. I'm probably somebody's patient, but not theirs.

I wander down a hall with numbered examination

rooms on both sides. Mr. Aidact and Mr. Perkins must be in one of these, but how do I find the right one?

Mr. Perkins is a crabby guy who knows nothing about field hockey, but I sure hope he's okay.

"There's no fracture," comes a voice from room 6. "I'll just tape you up and send you on your way."

I peek in the doorway, but the patient is a lady with a swollen ankle.

I'm leaving muddy footprints on the floor, and I feel bad for messing up a place that's supposed to be clean and sterile. That's when I realize that the prints up ahead can't be mine. I haven't gone that far yet. They must have come from somebody else with muddy shoes.

Of course! Mr. Aidact.

I follow the mud spots. They lead up the hall and directly into room 11.

Carefully, I peer in through the doorway. Mr. Perkins is sitting upright on the exam table. He's wrapped in blankets, and there's a thick bandage on his forehead, but his eyes are open, he's speaking, and he looks fine. Mr. Aidact is standing opposite him in that weird way he has—absolutely unmoving, still as a statue.

Should I go in? Probably not. I'm not supposed to be here at all.

I'm pondering what to do when a doctor breezes past

me into the room. "It seems to be a slight concussion—"

As he approaches the patient, Mr. Aidact backs out of the way, accidentally stepping onto the electronic scale.

My eyes are riveted on the readout. Either the scale is broken, or my teacher weighs *576 pounds*!

Shocked, I stagger back, almost as if somebody shoved me. I manage a couple of steps and collide with a nurse, who keeps me upright while also juggling a tray of stainless steel instruments.

"Sorry," I mumble.

She takes in my mud-smeared state and assumes I'm a patient. "What room are you in?"

"No room," I try to explain. "My teacher—I mean my *student* teacher—"

She takes my arm and steers me toward the exit. "Out of here. Now."

I stumble along, racking my brain for excuses, but only one thought registers with me: *576 pounds . . . 576 pounds . . . Mr. Aidact weighs 576 pounds. . . .*

Then I'm in the waiting room and the heavy doors are shutting behind me. Through the floor-to-ceiling windows, I can see Mrs. Berg loading up the bus again, and she's frantic about something. I run outside.

"Fifty-three!" she's exclaiming in agitation. "There

were fifty-four of us at Hickenlooper! Who's missing?"

"It's okay, Mrs. Berg," I call. "It's just me. But we can't go yet. Mr. Aidact and Mr. Perkins are still inside. Good news—Mr. Perkins is okay."

Ainsley catches me up. Our driver had to Uber here so he can bring us back to school. We're not waiting for Mr. Perkins and Mr. Aidact. Principal Candiotti is coming for them with her car.

I practically fall into the empty seat across the aisle from Oliver and Nathan.

"Long day?" Oliver asks with a sympathetic grin.

"Our teacher weighs five hundred and seventy-six pounds!" I burst out.

As soon as the words are out of my mouth, it just hits me. The buzz about a robot teacher—it's *true*! But it isn't Mrs. Berg or any of the others! It's Mr. Aidact!

I can't believe I didn't see it before. It's been right in front of my eyes. His instant knowledge of absolutely everything. The fact that nobody's ever seen him eat or drink and that he doesn't move a muscle when he stands still, like he's turned himself off or something. His strength—he hit a hockey ball off the field house that traveled three hundred yards through the air and still had the power to break a windshield. And his "student teacher"—I think of the strange metal instruments inside the giant briefcase. Those must be robot-fixing tools!

"Mr. Aidact is a robot," I barely whisper.

And what's their reaction: Shock? Amazement? Disbelief?

"Shhh," Oliver hisses.

"You *knew*?" I exclaim, struggling to keep my voice low. "How could you know?"

"We spied on him," Nathan admits. "He has—panels. He looks like a computer inside."

"He's a Department of Education project," Oliver adds. "Project AIDACT—it stands for Artificially Intelligent Designated Android Classroom Teacher. We found the whole plan on this old website. They told the faculty but nobody else."

"And you just sat on this little piece of information," I accuse. "You didn't think anybody else might need to know. He's my teacher too—and my coach!"

The coaching—how could I miss it? A guy with zero experience somehow turns a collection of amateurs who don't know which end of the stick to hold into a team competing for a state championship. Every time he switched our positions, he turned out to be 100 percent right, always maximizing each girl's talents with the job she had to do. Every new attack he designed worked like a charm—almost like he could see it playing out in his mind. Because he *could*! His mind *isn't* a mind; it's a computer!

"The Department of Education is trying to keep it secret," Oliver explains. "We didn't want to go up against them. Besides, would you have believed us if we told you?"

He's got a point. Something like this is almost impossible to swallow even when I've seen hard evidence. I never could have accepted it from a couple of clowns like Oliver and Nathan.

"You still could have warned me," I say resentfully. "If he stepped on my foot, he would have shattered every single one of my toes."

"We never knew how much he weighs," Oliver admits. "Although now that you mention it, I saw the Prius running a little lopsided with Mr. Aidact in the passenger seat."

All the way back to Brightling, my mind feels like a bag of microwave popcorn—ideas heating up, exploding, filling my brain to bursting. Mr. Aidact isn't human. My teacher; my coach—a machine. A fancy, sophisticated one, but a machine just the same.

Every time he calls me Rosalie, he's using the name that he learned through his artificial intelligence. He doesn't know me; facial recognition software compares my image to others in his database. I replay every interaction I've ever had with him, dating back to the first day of school, when he caught Oliver's spitball. None of it was real. All those weeks—a lie. You build up a relationship with a teacher. And mine turns out to be an un-person.

It hurts the most with the Bobcats. We're all so close to the coach—at least we thought we were. When he took over, we were just a bunch of clueless nobodies. I only signed on to pad my résumé. He built us into a real team. What was all that—a computer algorithm? When he got thrown out of our first game and had to watch from the roof of our bus in the parking lot—did his programming make him do that? When he celebrates with us, fights at our side, suffers along with every bruised knee and twisted ankle, is it all because some chip somewhere is telling him what to "feel"?

Of course it is. Machines can't "feel" anything. Mr. Aidact isn't any more human than a dishwasher or a microwave oven. He's convincing. I'll give him that. The Department of Education built a very believable robot. He sure fooled me. He fooled everybody. But once you *know*, you can never go back.

How are the other girls going to react when this

news reaches them? The team is undefeated. We're on an eleven-game winning streak after that opening-game tie. In two weeks, we play the Seahawks again in the championship game. We're *that* close to replacing the trophy that was stolen on Halloween. What will happen to the Bobcats when everybody learns the truth?

We're the same players. Cassidy bagging goals; Leticia defending our net; the rest of us doing our jobs and getting better every week. But everything will be different now. It was against the Sheridan Seahawks that we dug ourselves out of a 6–0 hole because Coach Aidact brought us back with the sheer force of his heart. Or so we thought.

When the news gets around that he doesn't have a heart, what then?

When we finally pull up in front of Brightling, Nathan asks in a small voice, "Are you going to tell anybody?"

I'm tempted to say yes purely as an in-your-face to those guys. If there's anybody at Brightling who doesn't deserve loyalty from me, it has to be Oliver and Nathan. But do I want to be like Kevin, spilling the beans about everything because I'm incapable of keeping the slightest secret?

I shake my head in resignation. "It doesn't matter. If

we figured it out, other people will too. A five-hundred-seventy-six-pound teacher is hard to hide."

The rain has stopped, and I'm actually looking forward to the walk home. Maybe it'll give me a chance to clear my head. But when I get off the bus, there's Mom.

"Hi, honey," she greets me. "How was orienteering?"

"It was a disaster," I inform her.

"That's nice." She's not listening, watching the people behind me filing down the bus steps.

Just as I suspected: she's hoping to "run into" Mr. Aidact.

That's the worst part of all this! It's awful enough that my teacher is a robot, but my mother has a crush on the guy!

"I see Mrs. Berg," Mom observes, "but didn't Mr. Aidact go too? Where is he?"

"The hospital," I reply tersely.

"The hospital? Is he hurt?"

I have to hold myself back from saying that nothing can hurt Mr. Aidact—nothing that a hospital can fix, anyway. Elon Musk, maybe. Not a doctor.

I bite my tongue. "His student teacher got a concussion. Orienteering isn't for tourists, you know."

For the first time, she takes in the state of my clothes. "I can see that. I guess I'd better get you home to the laundry. I'm not sure those shoes can be saved, though."

All the way in the car, she pushes me for information. "Poor Mr. Aidact. He must have been very upset that Mr. Perkins got injured."

"Don't worry about Mr. Aidact," I reply. "He doesn't take things too hard."

"You don't know Mr. Aidact like I do," she insists. "He may seem cool and distant on the surface, but deep down, he's very sensitive. He'd feel terrible if anything happened to his student teacher."

I don't know whether to laugh or scream. "If there's one word you should never use when you're talking about Mr. Aidact, it's *feel*."

"Rosalie, what are you talking about?"

We pull into the driveway. Without answering, I jump out of the car and storm into the house.

Mom is hot on my heels. "I know this isn't the kind of thing a young girl expects to hear from her mother. But I'm a single woman now, and I think Mr. Aidact and I might have a connection."

I just lose it. "No! There is no connection! Zero! There is absolutely nothing between you and Mr. Aidact!"

I try to run away, but she grabs my wrist and wheels me around. "Rosalie, we need to talk." Her expression is all sympathy and compassion. She thinks I'm upset that she wants to start dating again! How can I make her see that the problem is a lot more basic than that? "I'm an adult. I think I know more about this relationship than you do."

"Trust me—you don't—"

She's beginning to lose patience. "Give me one reason why Mr. Aidact and I—"

"*Because he's a robot!*" I blurt at the top of my lungs.

"Honey, that's an unkind thing to say. He may be a little standoffish—"

Once the floodgates are open, it comes pouring out. "It's not unkind—it's true! He's a real robot, like C-3PO and WALL-E! He's a pilot project from the Department of Education to create an android teacher! He has more in common with the toaster than he has with you! You can't have a relationship with him because he isn't human!"

I pause to catch my breath, panting like I've just run a marathon.

My mother is staring at me in wide-eyed shock.

CONFIDENTIAL REPORT

To: Department of Education, Washington, DC
From: Paul Perkins, PE
Project: AIDACT

Recent alarming events have caused me to question the workability of the entire AIDACT project. On a school field trip, the unit took several extraordinary actions, none of which could have been predicted by the Department of Education. In each case, AIDACT was protecting students and/or the project engineer from harm. In that way, the unit's decisions were correct. But because the situation was so far from anything we could have planned for, I question whether we can ever safely say that an AIDACT unit is truly under control. At one point, the unit operated a motor vehicle full of passengers. As it turned out, AIDACT did well. Still, the mere fact that we didn't know that until it was actually happening is deeply disturbing.

The project is on very thin ice now. We must watch carefully and be ready to shut it down at the first sign of trouble.

PROJECT STATUS: Yellow
SPECIAL EXPENSES
See attached file—medical bills

Principal Candiotti

The trouble started a week and a half ago when a parent called to complain about Syesha Berg.

I assured him that Mrs. Berg is one of my most experienced educators. Nobody ever complains about Syesha. Well, that's not technically true. The students have a lot to say about her endless lectures and her droning monotone voice. But she's a nationally certified teacher with two master's degrees.

"That's not what I heard," the concerned father grumbled.

"Exactly what did you hear?"

"Okay—this might sound a little out-there. But the

kids are saying that she's—inhuman."

"I beg your pardon?"

"Well, not *in*human. More like *non*human."

"Nonhuman?"

"Like—a robot."

And there it was.

What could I do? I gave him my absolute assurance that Syesha is quite human and finished the conversation by adding, "You know how it is with rumors in a middle school." Then I hung up, sat back in my chair, and gazed out the window at my view of the ravine.

It wasn't so much what I said to that father as what I *didn't* say. I didn't tell him that while Mrs. Berg is *not* a robot, we just so happen to have another teacher who *is*.

So I'm in it now. If there's one parent, there will be five by the end of the day, and fifty by the end of the week. And by the second week, it'll be all of them. And they won't just be asking about Mrs. Berg or Ms. Muro or Mr. Zelcer. They'll *know*. Pretty soon they'll be an angry mob surrounding the school, waving torches and pitchforks.

The angry mob comes in the form of our PTA president, Peggy Arnette. Her daughter, Rosalie, is in Mr. Aidact's homeroom and is one of his field hockey players. I actually thought Peggy liked Mr. Aidact. She always spoke very highly of him to me.

Well, that's over.

She catches me at a hectic time. It's the evening of the field trip to the Hickenlooper Center. I've just gotten home from picking up Mr. Aidact and Paul Perkins from Mercy Hospital, so it's been a marathon day when she calls my cell phone.

"A *robot*?" she shrills. "Mr. Aidact is a robot and you didn't tell anybody? Not even the *PTA*?"

"Calm down, Peggy," I try to soothe, but I'm even less calm than she is at this point. I've known this moment would come ever since I got off the phone with that irate dad. And even though I've had plenty of time to prepare, I'm just not ready for it. "Our school was chosen out of every middle school in the country for this special project. I wish I could say more, but secrecy was one of the conditions."

"No wonder!" she raves. "It's a disgrace!"

"It's a rare opportunity," I argue. "Mr. Aidact is very popular! Did you know that the students voted him Brightling Teacher of the Year?"

"I don't care if they voted him Motor Trend Car of the Year," she snarls.

"And surely Rosalie has told you what a wonderful coach he is," I press on. "The girls are only one win away from a state championship. That hasn't happened since 1974!"

"I want him gone," she says firmly.

"Not possible," I insist. "The school board made an agreement with the Department of Education."

"The school board thinks it runs things, but it doesn't," she informs me. "It's the parents who are in charge of a school. I'm going to make sure that every single family knows their children are being taught by an unfeeling piece of technology. We'll see who's Teacher of the Year then!" And she hangs up on me.

I sit on my couch for a long time, hyperventilating. Now what? Now what? I can't even imagine the firestorm that's going to hit my office tomorrow.

Maybe I'll take a sick day. It's not unheard of to cut school when you feel overwhelmed.

But you can't do that when you're the principal.

It starts early the next morning. By the time I get to school, there are sticky notes covering the entire surface of my desk. I shuffle the mouse to bring my computer out of hibernation. I have 211 unread emails.

My secretary appears in the doorway. "Channel Four News is on the phone. What should I tell them?"

My mind reels. Among the parent emails, there are messages from reporters and bloggers, even *Educator's Digest*. How long have I dreamed about the wonderful day when Project AIDACT would finally become public and Brightling would get credit for hosting such a groundbreaking experiment? Now it's happened, and there's nothing wonderful about it. The whole world is pressing to interview me, and all I want is to be left alone.

"Take a message!" I exclaim. "Take messages from everybody. As far as you know, I'm out of the office all day!" And to back up this claim, I march out the door. Destination: the seventh-grade wing.

The halls are crowded with students arriving and heading for their lockers. It's a loud, rambunctious time. Within reason, I'm fine with it. It's my policy to let kids be kids as they transition to the learning portion of the day.

But outside room 233, the corridor is quiet as a tomb. Mr. Aidact stands at his door, his hand raised in the high-five position that students used to line up to slap. Now he has no takers. The kids who used to jostle each other to get close to him cross the hall and hug the opposite wall just to avoid him. There's no hustle and bustle here, only awkward silence. Fans who competed for his attention just yesterday won't even meet his eyes.

Steinke Newhouse is directly in front of me. As he approaches the doorway, Mr. Aidact tosses out, *"What's poppin'?"*

Steinke deliberately looks away and keeps on walking.

So the word is out. It was all fun and games when it was wild speculation about Syesha. But now that it's official—now that the real robot has a name and face—everything's changed. Kids pick up on the anxiety and suspicion that they see in their parents. And suddenly, Mr. Aidact is someone to be avoided, maybe feared.

So help me, I actually experience a pang of sympathy to see one of my teachers so ignored, so rejected. I even fancy that I detect a hurt expression on his face. It's impossible. A machine has no feelings. And his arm will never get tired no matter how long he leaves his hand up there, waiting for a high five that's never going to come.

"Good morning, Principal Candiotti."

No, that isn't wistful sadness in his voice. There's no human emotion in his tone. *I'm* the one providing the human emotion. He's greeting me the way he always does.

"Good morning, Mr. Aidact. Good morning, Paul."

Paul Perkins is perched on a desk, his large case balanced on his lap. The project engineer doesn't look well at all. No wonder. His bruise has bloomed beyond the bandage on his forehead, and his skin is pale and waxy.

"The jig is up, Paul," I say quietly. "The kids know. The parents are in revolt. The media is waiting for a statement. What does the Department of Education want me to tell them?"

He shrugs helplessly. "I have no idea. I'm just an engineer. I'm in charge of the technological part of the AIDACT project. I don't have anything to do with public relations."

It's what I expected him to say, but it's still a bitter pill to swallow. It means that all this is *my* problem.

✳

I go back to the office and return a few of the parent calls. The day doesn't get any better. My right ear throbs from being yelled at. I switch the phone to the left. Pretty soon it throbs too.

The complaints stack up: How could I allow such a thing to happen at Brightling? Why didn't I inform the parents? How could I let my students be taught by someone who doesn't have a soul? Who do I think I am, anyway?

Parents threaten to homeschool their kids or send them to private schools. Some of them talk about suing the district or withholding their taxes.

Just to get away from the phone, I make several trips to room 233 to check on Mr. Aidact. He's teaching to half-empty rooms. A check of the roll shows that a lot of his students are absent today, kept home by their parents. Those who do attend his classes are staring blankly straight ahead or looking deliberately away from the teacher.

I also visit the cafeteria during his lunch period. It's normally a free-for-all. At any given time, there would be at least a dozen hands in the air—everybody yammering for Mr. Aidact's attention. He'd scramble from table to table to reach his fans, all of them determined to stump him with a trivia question or hip-hop rhyme. Howls of gleeful outrage would ring out when he'd come up with the answers—because he always came up with the answers. The cavernous room would echo with applause and cheers.

I didn't love the noise. But the silence feels wrong too—so many faces studiously buried in trays and brown bags. I speak from personal experience when I say that the chicken nuggets we serve at Brightling don't deserve that kind of devotion.

What must Mr. Aidact think of all this, as he walks between the long tables, waiting for the calls and waves that are no longer incoming? Well, maybe *think* isn't the right word, but surely his AI notices that something is different.

I go back to my parent calls, which keep me busy for the rest of the school day. That's when Mr. Aidact hails me through the intercom system.

"What can I do for you, Mr. Aidact?" I ask warily.

"Nobody's here," he informs me. "In detention. Where are all the pupils?"

"Maybe nobody's in detention today," I suggest. But as soon as the words pass my lips, I realize how ridiculous they are. Steinke is *always* in detention. And Mia—I seem to remember her rolling up to school twenty-five minutes into first period.

I conjure a picture of the hall outside detention. Students packed belly to belly, jockeying for position to be the first inside when the three thirty bell sounds— to score the best seats, to capture a little more of their hero's precious time. Mr. Aidact's fans come from every grade, clique, and corner of the school, from athletes to outcasts, from emo kids to metal heads to skateboarders to the beautiful and popular. Detention hasn't really been detention for quite some time here.

At least until today.

I pause at the intercom, waiting for him to reason it out. His processors can sift through the collected knowledge of humankind in a matter of seconds, but he doesn't seem to be capable of understanding this. Maybe that's because he's always known exactly what he is, so why would anybody make a big deal out of it?

"I'll be right there," I tell him, and head down the hall.

Mr. Aidact stands outside room 233, looking back and forth down the corridor, still waiting for the crowd. I can't help picturing a camera pivoting on a tripod. Even more strangely, I feel guilty for thinking of him that way.

Paul is seated at the teacher's desk, watching his charge and writing in his notebook. I'm almost tempted to slap him for showing no sympathy for a coworker in distress.

I try to be businesslike. "I don't think anyone's coming, Mr. Aidact."

I can't escape the sense that he's upset, even though I know he isn't.

He says, "I don't understand why the pupils are avoiding me. It's—wack."

I swallow a lump in my throat. "I don't think they mean anything by it. They found out you're—what you are. People often have trouble dealing with someone who's—" My voice trails off under his piercing blue gaze.

He tilts his head in that way he has. "I understand," he announces finally. "It's because I'm—different."

Paul is amazed. "You learned that from the internet?"

"Not directly," Mr. Aidact explains. "But I accessed a database of books and movies. It's a common theme among humans."

"Well, no sense wasting your time here," I forge on. "Get an early start on field hockey practice. Don't forget, the big game is coming."

It must be the right thing to say because he turns his back on me and strides away. Paul scrambles to keep up with him. I bring up the rear.

We follow Mr. Aidact down the stairs and out to the athletic field. I hug my blazer around me in the chilly late-autumn breeze. It's something I remember from my own field hockey days. The season stretches into early December. By the time the championship is determined, the weather has turned cold.

The first thing I notice is that the Bobcats aren't in practice gear yet, which I assume is because we're early.

Then I see the lineup of cars in the parking lot—mothers and fathers beckoning and honking.

The players stand in a group, caught between the urgent signals from their parents and their loyalty to their beloved coach—who has suddenly transformed into something odd, unacceptable, and even scary. The girls are torn, their expressions uneasy. They're not running for the parking lot, but they're edging away from Mr. Aidact's approach.

Out of the lead car jumps Peggy Arnette. She marches onto the turf, loaded for bear, her back ramrod-straight in a posture worthy of Mr. Aidact himself.

"Rosalie!" she calls. "We're leaving! Now!"

Rosalie doesn't answer, flinching uncomfortably on the windy field.

"*Rosalie!*" my PTA president all but snaps.

Mr. Aidact speaks up. "Mrs. Arnette—"

"*Don't* speak to me!" She turns on him. "You've got some nerve pretending to be something you're not. You may be hot stuff at Dave and Buster's, but you're nothing but a big phony!" And she marches away, dragging Rosalie by the arm.

The girl is distraught. "Sorry, Coach," she tosses over her shoulder.

As they approach the parking lot, the line of cars breaks into a cacophony of impatient honking.

That shatters whatever resistance is left. The other Bobcats offer tearful apologies and slink off toward their parents.

I can't quite explain why, but it's the saddest thing I've ever seen in my career as an educator. A principal should be able to defuse situations like this, make things better.

Instead, I've never felt so helpless.

CONFIDENTIAL REPORT

To: Department of Education, Washington, DC
From: Paul Perkins, PE
Project: AIDACT

Now that AIDACT's identity has been revealed, the entire school community is in full revolution. Parents are angry at being kept in the dark, and their children now regard AIDACT as suspicious, alien, and possibly even dangerous. There is no way the unit can be an effective teacher under these circumstances—especially since the AI system is dragging AIDACT inexorably toward a mental age of twelve.

Recommendation: The project should be canceled at Brightling. The unit should be deactivated, and its memory wiped clean.

PROJECT STATUS: Red

SPECIAL EXPENSES
Moving costs back to Washington

Oliver Zahn

I've never been a huge fan of school, but the one thing that makes it bearable is the laughing. Stick eight hundred kids in the same building, throw in teachers, principals, librarians, guidance counselors, custodians, and lunch ladies, and funny stuff is bound to happen. Can you imagine how boring it would be to take a school and suck out all the humor?

Guess what—that just happened here at Brightling. Ever since the news got around that Mr. Aidact isn't human, Brightling has been as funny as an open grave.

So we have a robot teacher. So what? Well, parents aren't too big on that. As a matter of fact, they're totally losing their minds over it. The teachers are uptight, since they're who everybody's so mad at. They're the ones who knew about Mr. Aidact all along—them and Principal Candiotti. Our parents are ticked off because the school used us as guinea pigs in an experiment. The principal is blaming the whole thing on the Department of Education, who made them keep everything secret. And who's caught in the middle? The kids. That leaves us slogging along in a place where you can go a whole day without hearing so much as a snicker.

It's torture for a guy like me. So when the paper slips out of Perkins's notebook and flutters down the stairwell to land at my feet, I grab it like a drowning sailor holds on to a life preserver.

"What's that?" Nathan asks.

"I don't even care," I tell him stubbornly. "Whatever it is, I'm going to make it into a spitball the size of a Smart car. I'm going to get some fun out of this joyless, sad-sack school by spitballing a fake student teacher with his own paper."

Nathan takes the sheet from me and scans it as we make our way up the stairs. By the time we reach the second floor, all the color has drained from his face.

"You'd better read this," he hisses, thrusting the page into my hands.

It isn't funny. That goes without saying. It's worse than not funny. It's awful.

The paper is a printed email from the Department of Education:

TO: PerkinsPE@EdDept.gov
RE: Project AIDACT

Paul—we agree with your assessment that the project must be ended. An engineering team will be coming by noon on Saturday, December 3, to assist you. They will have the codes to shut AIDACT down and erase all memory and programming. It has been decided that the unit will be taken out of service and shipped back to the DC lab to be salvaged for spare parts. . . .

I don't think I've ever been so shocked—not even when those high school kids jumped us in the sandpit on Halloween. "Spare parts?" I rasp. "That's like—murder!"

Nathan holds up a hand. "Seems to me you can't murder someone who isn't really alive."

"Of course he's alive!" I rant. "Okay, maybe not in the usual way, but he's got a lot more personality than half the teachers in this place! And he's smarter than all of them put together!"

"You're right," Nathan says breathlessly. "Before the news got out that he runs on batteries, kids voted him Teacher of the Year!"

"When does a machine start to be a real person?" I rave on. "Mr. Aidact *cares* about people. He cares about Stinky and Mia, and *nobody* cares about them. He waded through a river to rescue us at the Hickenlooper Center. You think a bunch of robot designers programmed him to do that? No—he did it because he *wanted* to. And when Perkins had to get to the hospital, he taught himself to drive a bus because he was worried about the guy. You don't get much more human than that."

Nathan nods thoughtfully. "He's a piece of technology, but when you're face-to-face with him, that's not how it feels."

"Wiping his memory, breaking him down for spare parts. What's next, huh? The guillotine? No way—not going to happen."

"But what can we do about it?" Nathan laments. "They're the Department of Education—the government. We're just kids. How can we rescue a doomed robot?"

When the answer comes to me, it's the most natural thing in the world. "We don't have to rescue him. We just have to tip him off."

Nathan stares. "What do you mean, 'tip him off'?"

"Simple," I explain. "The government is coming for him on Saturday. So he has until Friday to get out of here."

"But—" He's shocked. "Can a robot do that?"

I shrug. "He's got legs. He can run away. He weighs almost six hundred pounds, so I pity the guy who tries to stop him. And he's got the whole internet in his head, so he can learn pretty much anything."

"Yeah, but where's he going to *go*?" Nathan challenges. "His world revolves around Perkins. Can he even make it on his own?"

"I'm not saying it won't be *hard*. But it's got to be better than being turned into spare parts. First let him escape. Then he can worry about the details. Maybe his AI will show him what to do. It always has before."

The only place to talk to Mr. Aidact without his student teacher/engineer nosing around is in the cafeteria. Perkins eats, while his robot charge prefers to stay in the main lunchroom, where the kids are.

It used to be almost impossible to get his attention. Now everybody ignores him, not even glancing up when he walks by. You've never seen so many faces concentrating so totally on so much gross cafeteria food.

If that bugs Mr. Aidact, he doesn't show it. But the

minute Nathan and I invite him to join us, he's at our side. "What can I do for you pupils?"

I don't bother with a lot of buildup. All the secrets are out now—both what he is and the fact that everybody knows about it. So I push the printed email across the table. "This fell out of Mr. Perkins's notebook."

He reads it, hands it back to me, and repeats, "What can I do for you pupils?"

"Mr. Aidact!" Nathan blurts. "Don't you understand? They're going to turn you off!"

"Oh, yes," he confirms. "The message is clear. That's the sitch." These days, Mr. Aidact goes back and forth between sounding like a teacher and sounding like a kid.

"Don't you even *care*?" I demand.

"I'm not a biological life-form," he explains reasonably. "I was designed for Project AIDACT. Project AIDACT is over, which means *I* am over."

"You knew about this?" Nathan asks in amazement.

"No one actually told me. There was no reason to. I was designed for a purpose, and that purpose no longer exists."

"That's where you're wrong!" I shoot back, a little surprised at how angry I feel. "Project AIDACT was *one* purpose, but it wasn't all of them. What about the Bobcats and the Trivia Club and all those kids who used to pack into detention? And that's just what you've accomplished already. If you get deactivated, we lose not just what you've done but everything you're ever going to do. So you can't tell me your purpose is over. Your purpose is just starting!"

Mr. Aidact tilts his head the way he always does when he's using his internet connection. Nathan and I wait for him to come out of it, but whatever data he's sifting through, there must be an awful lot of it. The bell rings. Students bus their trays, gather their stuff, and head for sixth period, but we're still sitting there, waiting to hear what Mr. Aidact has to say. What research, what analysis could possibly be keeping the robot teacher's computer brain tied up for so long?

At last he returns to himself and fixes us with his steady blue gaze. If he notices that the entire cafeteria cleared out while he was lost in the web, he doesn't mention it.

"Wow," Nathan breathes. "That was the longest one ever! What were you thinking about?"

"Dying," he replies mildly. "You humans spend a lot of time talking about it. It's in books, movies, plays, poems, legends, and songs. I never believed it applied to me, but now I see that's wrong. An AIDACT unit is designed to make choices."

"And?" I prompt breathlessly.

"I choose not to be deactivated."

The two of us jump up and high-five him across the table. For the record, it feels just like slapping hands with a regular flesh-and-blood person.

"Way to go, Mr. Aidact!" I cheer. "No surrender!"

He nods. "I'll discuss it with Mr. Perkins. He'll know what to do."

"No!" Nathan is horrified.

"He's on *their* side," I explain. "The government. They're the ones who want to turn you off in the first place. If this is going to work, you have to sneak away behind their backs."

"That's not part of my programming," he points out.

"Neither is driving a bus," I argue. "But when you needed it to happen, you made it part of your programming."

"That was officially logged as a software glitch," he confesses.

"That was no glitch!" Nathan exclaims. "You were awesome! There was no one to tell you what to do, and you rocked it!"

"I rocked it," he repeats, looking pleased.

"You totally pass as human," I go on. "You fooled eight hundred kids and their parents. You need to travel to a new town in a new state and start a new life. And this is important: you can't tell anybody what you are and where you came from."

"I'll be"—a quick head tilt—"living on the q.t."

"Hiding out from the Department of Education," Nathan confirms. "I wonder if anybody's ever done that before."

"And where is this new town of hiding out?" he asks.

"Anywhere," I reply. "The farther the better. How do you feel about Colorado?"

"The cold, dry air would be excellent for my circuits," he approves. "No condensation. When exactly am I making this move?"

"As soon as possible," I say positively. "You have to be gone before that engineering team comes for you."

"Absolutely not. The state championship game is on Saturday. I can't abandon my players."

"But your players abandoned *you!*" Nathan puts in. "Nobody comes to practice anymore. You don't know if they're even going to show up on Saturday!"

"If they do show up," he returns evenly, "their coach will be there."

"But the game is Saturday," I protest. "That's the day they're coming for you!"

He's adamant. "An AIDACT unit is, first and

foremost, a teacher. Nothing is more important than your pupils."

"Not even your life?" Nathan demands.

Mr. Aidact doesn't answer. Nathan and I stare at each other. It's a miracle that we've managed to persuade Mr. Aidact that he has to escape. But this last bit might be asking too much. As human as Mr. Aidact can be, he's still a machine. And no one can convince a machine to go against its main programming. If he thinks he has to be there for the Bobcats, we'll never change his mind.

I turn back to Mr. Aidact. "If we can come up with a way to sneak you out of town after the game on Saturday, do you promise to go?"

"Word," he confirms.

I swallow hard. It's going to take all my skills as a rule-wrecker to pull this off.

Rosalie Arnette

I can't shake the feeling that this is all my fault. I'm the one who let myself get mad enough to tell Mom she was romancing a robot in her own mind.

Note to self: don't ever do that again. For someone who used to think she could plan out her entire future, I've sure been flying by the seat of my pants lately.

Now Mr. Aidact is public enemy number one. If parents are being jerks, their kids are just as bad, treating our teacher like he's a coffee maker or an electric can opener—a brainless machine.

The Bobcats are the worst of all. We owe him everything. He took a bunch of newbies and randos and turned us into a powerhouse that's playing for the state championship on Saturday. Except that nobody even goes to practice anymore because their parents won't let them. As for the game—well, I don't think we have much of a chance to win without any players. There goes Mrs. Candiotti's only chance to replace the trophy that got stolen. Then again, she's the principal, so she's part of the scam to keep Mr. Aidact secret—which is what everybody's so upset about in the first place.

I admit it. I'm in a lousy mood. Sure, we're all responsible for maintaining a positive outlook, but life has to meet you halfway, doesn't it? And it doesn't help that I've just made it to my locker this morning and already here come Oliver and Nathan. That can't be good news. It never is.

I stick out my chin at them. "What?"

Oliver doesn't reply—which instantly proves that something huge is going on. Oliver has plenty to say about everything. So his silence now speaks textbooks. He hands me a piece of paper.

TO: PerkinsPE@EdDept.gov
RE: Project AIDACT

"How did you get this?" I demand. "You're not supposed to have it."

"Read it," Nathan insists.

So I do. It's an email from the Department of Education saying that Mr. Aidact is going to be shut down and dismantled into spare parts.

It's a miracle that I don't pass out on the spot, right there in front of my locker. I've always had mixed feelings about Mr. Aidact. I thought he was kind of an oddball—and that turned out to be a million percent spot on. He's a fantastic coach, a pretty good teacher, and a handy person to have around when you need to cross a river. On the other hand, it's hard to warm up to the guy your mom has a crush on—and that's even before you find out the guy isn't really a guy at all.

"Can they do this?" I half whisper.

"They can and they will," Oliver replies. "Technically, he's not a person. He's their property."

As soon as the words are out of his mouth, I know it's true, and there's no way for us to stop it. And like a baby, I start crying—right in front of those two dipsticks. "He *is* a person! He's *our* person! And we're his pupils!"

They don't make fun of me. In fact, they look like they want to cry too. That alone proves how awful this is—that the kings of comedy can't find anything funny about it.

"We might have a plan," Nathan offers.

I jump straight down his throat. "You should have said that first! What is it?"

Their plan seems impossible at first, but it starts to make sense the more you think about it. Mr. Aidact is built and programmed to seem human, so he can live anywhere as just a regular person. So all he has to do is get out of town before the engineering team comes to shut him off. I feel the first stirrings of hope since Oliver showed me that terrible email.

"So what's the problem?" I ask.

"He won't leave," Oliver explains. "Not till he coaches you guys in the championship game on Saturday."

Now that I've finally got the waterworks turned off, my eyes fill up again. "That's our coach," I quaver, tears spilling past my goofy grin. "He's risking his life for a team that isn't even playing for him anymore."

The idea is that as long as Mr. Aidact is coaching, the engineers won't be able to get close to him. Then, in the excitement of somebody winning the championship, we can sneak him out of there.

"The game is at Memorial Field, which is only a few blocks from the big bus station downtown," Nathan reasons. "We'll have the ticket bought in advance, and off he goes."

"But what if the game gets canceled?" I sniffle. "None

of the girls are even allowed to practice if Mr. Aidact is going to be there. We have no team."

"That's where rule-wrecking comes in," Oliver informs me. "Practice or no practice, there's no reason some of you can't sneak out to Memorial Field at ten a.m. on Saturday. It doesn't matter if you stink, but there has to be a game."

I stand up a little straighter. This—this could actually work! Oliver and his stupid rule-wrecking might be able to save Mr. Aidact! And me right in the middle of it!

I fold the printed email and stick it in my pocket.

"Hey, that's ours!" Nathan protests.

"I need it," I tell them. "If you want the team there on Saturday morning, we have to know what we're fighting for."

Nathan Popova

"Hey, Stinky—where are you going?"

Ever since Halloween, I can't look at Stinky without picturing those two letters across his forehead, even though any sign of them is long gone now.

"Home," he replies. "Nothing doing around here. They still haven't started detention back up since everybody found out about—you know."

"That's good news, right?" Oliver offers. "More free time for you."

"I hate free time," Stinky grumbles. "It's boring."

"I guess you miss Mr. Aidact, huh?" I say.

"Don't say that name!" he snaps. "I never want to

hear it again. That guy isn't Mr. anything except Mr. Faker! That's what I get for liking a teacher—lies."

"He never lied," Oliver points out. "Did he ever tell you he *wasn't* a robot?"

Stinky stops in the schoolyard and turns to face us. "I know what you're doing. You're trying to trick me into liking Mr. Aidact again. You even made me say his name!"

"You won't have to hear that name ever again after Saturday," Oliver assures him.

"Good." Stinky's eyes narrow under his unibrow. "Wait—why?"

I unfold a photocopy of the Department of Education email and hand it to him.

He scans it. "What does *salvaged* mean?"

"It means they're going to turn him off, take him apart, and use the pieces to build other stuff," Oliver explains.

The bushy brow shoots up to meet his hairline. "Can they do that? Isn't that against the law?"

"It should be," I agree sadly, "but it isn't."

"We have a plan to help Mr. Aidact escape before the Department of Education guys get to him," Oliver goes on. "Are you with us?"

"Yeah!" he exclaims in a belligerent tone. "What kind of jerk do you think I am? Mr. Aidact is the best teacher I ever had! No way am I going to let anybody do salvage on him!"

"Good," I say. "We need you in the audience at the girls' field hockey championship game. Memorial Field. Saturday—ten a.m."

"Didn't they cancel that?"

"That's what we want our parents to think," Oliver confides. "But Mr. Aidact set it up again with the league. The girls are going to play. Rosalie confirmed it with every single Bobcat."

Stinky is mystified. "How does me watching field hockey help Mr. Aidact?"

"When the game is over, we'll all rush the field," Oliver informs him. "And Mr. Aidact will slip away in the confusion."

"And he's going to do it?" Stinky marvels. "It doesn't sound very teacher-like."

"He has no choice," I assure him. "It's a matter of life and—salvage."

✳

"Figures." Mia Spinelli hands the photocopied email back to me. "You get a month of detentions for a few late slips, but the government is stripping people for spare parts, and that's fine."

"So you'll help us?" I prompt.

She nods. "Mr. Aidact really listened to me. Out of everybody in this town, he's the most human. Not like Darryl. Someone should break *him* down for spare parts."

"Tell all your friends," Oliver puts in. "We need a big crowd for a big distraction. But no parents. This is kids only. Nobody over fourteen is allowed to know about it. And remember: game time is nine a.m. sharp."

She thanks us and promises to be there.

I'm confused about something. "Why'd you say nine a.m.? The game doesn't start until ten."

He shrugs. "It's Mia. If I tell her ten, she won't get there till after lunch."

That's how we spend the rest of the week, spreading the word about the plot against Mr. Aidact. As funny as everyone feels about the robot thing, nobody thinks it's okay for the Department of Education to shut him off and dismantle him like he's trash.

"At first, kids overreacted because their parents did," Oliver comments as we make our way home on Thursday. "But as soon as they calm down, they see how awful this is."

I nod. "We're more comfortable with technology. You should see my dad when there's a Windows update on his computer. It's like World War Three." My house comes into view as we round the corner. "I feel like we've talked to half the school, and they talked to the other half. But it's impossible to know for sure if we're going to get the kind of crowd we need. What if nobody shows up and Mr. Aidact gets caught?"

"We did everything we could," Oliver soothes.

"What about Krumlich?" I remind him. "We never brought him into this. When it comes to broadcasting a message, he's the champion."

He shakes his head vigorously. "There are two ways this plan can go wrong. One is a lousy turnout, and the other is if too many parents clue in. Telling Kevin is like going on Radio Free Europe. He'll blab to everyone, and pretty soon it'll reach the Bobcats' families. If it's game off, it's escape off too."

✳

Friday is the last chance to make sure that all the bases are covered for tomorrow. I know my Oliver Alert should be wailing like a banshee, but I can't worry about that. This is too important. We have to spend all day reaching out to people we might have missed. If we're going to save Mr. Aidact, everybody counts.

Darryl corners me in the boys' room. "Mia gave me all the details. I'll be there tomorrow."

"Mia?" I echo. "I thought things were—complicated between you guys."

He looks surprised. "How? We barely know each other. Actually, I was kind of thinking of asking her out. You know, after we save Mr. Aidact."

Just before third period, Avalon pulls Oliver and me down to the *Barker* offices. "I had an idea," she tells us proudly. "I'm printing up flyers to pass out at the game tomorrow. Then, when it's time for Mr. Aidact to disappear, we can all throw them up in the air."

"Perfect," Oliver approves. "Everyone's attention will be drawn up to the papers swirling in the wind. And when they look down again, Mr. Aidact will be gone."

"I came up with a great slogan." From the stack churning out of the laser printer, she holds up the top page. The message is in bright teal blue, the team color. It reads:

COACH AIDACT IS UNREAL

Oliver is beside himself. "I love it! I love it so much!"

"I thought of putting his picture on there," Avalon

explains, "but I didn't want it to turn out to be a wanted poster."

Lunch is the only time we can speak to Mr. Aidact without his student teacher nosing around. It's doubly important today, since we have to finalize our plans and make sure everybody's on the same page.

At our usual table, we wait for him to notice us and come by. Instead, he continues his patrol of the cafeteria. Kids are still ignoring him, even though most of them know about the plans for his big escape tomorrow. Furtive glances dart his way, but nobody speaks to him. The lunchroom is every bit as quiet as it's been since word got out that our new teacher is a robot.

Oliver has a different concern. "Why doesn't he come over and talk to us? Doesn't he want to make sure that tomorrow's still on?"

I'm horrified. "You don't think he forgot, do you?"

"The guy's a walking, talking hard drive! How could he forget?" As Mr. Aidact passes by us, Oliver gets a hand on the fabric of the teacher's sleeve and tugs him gently over to our table.

"What can I do for you pupils?" the teacher asks genially.

I can't hold back. "Don't you remember the *plan*?"

In answer, Mr. Aidact begins to recite the details.

"I go to Memorial Field at nine thirty. My team will be there. We play the game—"

"Fine—you remember," Oliver cuts him off. "But what if something goes wrong? For instance, what if Mr. Perkins gives you a hard time?"

"Oh, he won't," is the reply. "He's happy that the game is going to be played."

"Something's fishy," I tell Oliver. "Perkins is never happy about anything. Not a field hockey game. Probably not even winning the lottery. The guy's a total crab."

"There's one thing you have to do for me," Mr. Aidact tells us. "There is a GPS tracker located in a small port on my back. I can't reach it myself. Before the game, you'll have to remove it. Otherwise, wherever I go, they'll be able to find me."

Oliver and I exchange worried glances. We're just beginning to understand how complex this whole operation is going to be, and how easily it could fall apart.

"You've got it, Mr. Aidact," Oliver promises. "And if we strike oil in there, we'll split the profits with you, fifty-fifty."

"There are no fossil fuels anywhere in my body," the teacher replies seriously. "I am a zero-emissions unit, powered entirely by solar cells." He moves on to the next table.

"Good thing he told us about that tracker chip," I comment. "Mr. Aidact's pretty sharp."

"I guess," Oliver concedes. "But you'll notice I was right about him. No sense of humor. If he's the most advanced technology in the world, we've got a long way to go before they build a funny robot."

As the afternoon drags on, I find it harder and harder to pay attention in class. Just the idea of what we'll be trying to do tomorrow—and what will happen to Mr. Aidact if we fail—presses down on me like a weight. I keep thinking about the GPS chip and wondering how many details like that we might not know about. Any one of them could sink the whole plan.

Even Oliver seems stressed—and it takes a lot to worry Oliver. There are too many things that can go wrong.

Right before dismissal, Principal Candiotti comes on the PA system. *"Good afternoon. Before we break for the weekend, I'd like to offer congratulations to our very own Bobcats girls' field hockey team. Tomorrow would have been our shot at the state championship, but for various reasons, we have to forfeit. Girls, I don't want you to think for one second that you're not champions. That's partly my fault. I never should have made such a fuss about the championship trophy that was stolen. A trophy doesn't make you a champion. It's just a trinket. What makes you a champion is what's in your heart. Bobcats, you will always be our champions.*

"*I'd also like to offer my thanks to Mr. Aidact, who turned out to be a coach like no other.*" She pauses, and just for a second, I swear I hear her voice crack. "*We're thinking of you.*"

Rosalie Arnette

The teal and white of my uniform twirls behind the window of our dryer. It looks kind of like an exotic bird—but that's only because my eyes are rolling back in my head. This is the third time I've dozed off already—and that's just during the drying cycle. It's six a.m., and I've already been up for an hour, after a night where I barely slept at all. Instead of tossing and turning, why not wash my uniform so I can look good for Coach Aidact's last game?

Because that's what it is. It's the final game of the season, the match that will determine the state championship. And when it's done, one way or another, Mr. Aidact will be leaving.

About saving Mr. Aidact: We *have* to! Oh, I get that he's a robot and government property and all that. I don't care. He's a person, not a thing! And just because the idea comes from Oliver and Nathan doesn't mean it's wrong. Those two pinheads are wrong about everything else, but not this. That's why all the Bobcats agreed to sneak out this morning and play this game so we can help Mr. Aidact escape. He believed in us when we were less than nothing. And now we believe in him having a future— and that's a lot more important than field hockey.

I've never been so nervous in my life, and it has nothing to do with the game. Who cares about being state champions—except maybe Mrs. Candiotti? I'm scared because we all know what a long shot the escape is going to be. It's a life-and-death situation. If the Department of Education turns off Mr. Aidact, they're ending a life.

By the time Mom gets up around eight, the uniform is clean and dry and packed away in my gym bag. It, along with my cleats and field hockey stick, is hidden in the garage. Every Saturday at nine, Mom gets on Zoom with my aunt Jenny in Florida for a marathon yak session that lasts two hours minimum. Once that's underway, I text Mom that I'm going over to Leticia's to work on a school project. It's impossible—Leticia's an eighth grader, so we can't have any classes together. But I choose Leticia because her mother's not a member of the PTA, so Mom won't be able to find me.

Brightling isn't huge, but it's still a three-quarter-mile walk from my house to Memorial Field, which is right downtown. It's December now, and pretty chilly. I hug my fleece around me, but once the game starts, there'll be no protection from this biting wind.

I meet Darcy and Ainsley on the way, and the three of us run into Cassidy and Leticia.

I'm relieved. "I was afraid it was going to be just me this morning," I admit. "I thought everybody else might chicken out. Our parents are so dead set against Mr. Aidact."

"That's tough," Cassidy says with determination. "I wouldn't have cared if my folks put in a barbed-wire fence. Nothing was going to stop me from showing up for Coach."

There are grunts of agreement all around.

We pick up a few more team members on the walk, and by the time we approach the field, all the Bobcats are either marching with us or in view, coming by foot or bike.

The field is deserted except for a lone figure standing

on the home team bench, perfectly straight and still as a statue. We break into a run, cheering and punching at the air. Nobody's been to practice in more than a week, so he must have been wondering if we were going to show up at all.

Spying our approach, he jumps down and sprints to intercept us, crossing the field in a matter of seconds. It occurs to me that this is a five-hundred-plus-pound piece of machinery about to wipe us out before we can even put on cleats. But he stops short, and we swarm him. I don't think I've ever been so glad to see anybody.

The first thing I notice is that Mr. Perkins is nowhere to be found. I almost burst out: *Run, Mr. Aidact! Go now, while there's no one to stop you! Forget the game! Forget us! Save yourself!*

I remember what Oliver and Nathan said—that he could have taken off any time this week. But he wouldn't go because his Bobcats had one more game to play.

My heart swells, and I blurt, "We missed you, Mr. Aidact!"

And then we're all saying it, from the lowliest seventh graders right on up to team captain Cassidy.

"I noted the absence of you pupils as well." He adds, "It's cold today, so keep moving to stay warm."

We head for the field house to get changed.

Oliver Zahn

We watch as the twenty-dollar bill is sucked into the ticket machine. There's a clunking sound, and the bill comes right out again. The message on the screen reads: *REJECTED*. The amount paid stays at zero.

I flatten it against my chest, trying to smooth out all the crinkles. Then I reinsert it.

REJECTED.

"It's broken," Nathan complains.

"No, it isn't," I insist. "These machines are really finicky. The bills have to be perfectly flat."

It's a little after nine a.m., and we're in the Brightling bus station, buying a one-way ticket on the eleven forty-five express to Denver, Colorado. When the championship game is over, there won't be a spare minute for waiting at the ticket window. The timing will be crucial. Mr. Aidact needs to head straight for the bus and be gone.

"Why can't we just put it on my mom's credit card?" Nathan wheedles. "We can use the cash to pay her back."

"Great," I approve. "Have fun explaining to her why you spent a hundred bucks on a bus ticket. Plus credit cards are traceable. Do you want the government to figure out where Mr. Aidact is?"

Nathan gulps and produces a second twenty. "Try this one."

The machine swallows it right up.

The cash comes from everybody's lunch money, donated to Mr. Aidact's escape fund over the course of the week. By the end, we're stuffing quarters and even nickels into the machine, but we make it to the magic number of $102.50. The machine coughs up the ticket: DENVER, CO. The passenger name reads: Nathan Oliver.

Nathan points. "Why Nathan Oliver?"

I shrug. "I couldn't put Aidact. That's what the government will be looking for. Consider it a little tribute to the guys that made this escape possible." I stick the ticket in my pocket.

"I hope it *is* possible," Nathan mumbles anxiously.

"Right now it feels like a billion things have to go right for us to pull this off."

The station is just four blocks from Memorial Field. This is the distance Mr. Aidact has to cover to make it from the game to the bus. It doesn't seem that far—until you remember that the enemy is the United States government.

No—better not to think about that. This has to work.

As we enter the parking lot, Nathan grabs my arm and breathes, "Look!"

It's Perkins. Not unexpected—when you've got Mr. Aidact, his "student teacher" is never far away. But Perkins is standing with three big guys next to an unmarked cube van.

"That must be them," I whisper. "That team of engineers that's going to take Mr. Aidact away."

"Are we too late?" Nathan asks, his voice full of dread. "Is Mr. Aidact in the truck already?"

I scan the field. "No—there he is, running the girls through warm-ups. They're probably planning to grab him the minute the game ends."

Nathan slams his fist into his palm. "Not if we have anything to say about it!"

As we enter the field, I notice that the stands are already pretty full with kids wearing our team colors of teal and white. A lot of the students we recruited to come today are actually showing up—proof of just how much the robot teacher has come to mean to everybody. We'll need enough people to storm the field at the end of the game, so Mr. Aidact can get away in the confusion.

The place is filling even as we watch. Avalon stands at the main gate, handing out her MR. AIDACT IS UNREAL flyers to anyone who'll take them, even fans of the other team. I'm happy to note that some of our supporters are carrying large rolled-up posters. Nathan and I exchange a fist bump. Those will be another part of our plan later on.

Our opponents are the Sheridan Middle School Seahawks, the team we tied in the first game. Both schools have been undefeated since then, so the winner today will be state champions.

The two teams' fan bases couldn't be more different. The Seahawks' supporters are mostly adults—parents and staff members. They seem surprised at our big turnout— especially since it's 100 percent kids. *Our* teachers and parents have no idea this game is even being played. Rule number one: if you can't slip away unnoticed, don't come.

Mr. Aidact is with Leticia and a couple of the backs, working on defending penalty corners, when we approach.

"Good morning, pupils," he greets us.

"All right, Mr. Aidact," I say. "We're ready to help you with that little back problem."

Rosalie frowns. "He can't get a backache—can he?"

Mr. Aidact follows us into the field house, and we slip into the storage closet between the two locker rooms. The "back problem" is code for the GPS chip we have to get rid of so no one will be able to track him after he makes his escape.

Nathan shines his phone's flashlight while I pry open a small compartment between Mr. Aidact's shoulder blades using the nail file on my key chain. Even though we already witnessed it that day through the Submarine Commander periscope, don't let anyone ever tell you that it isn't plenty weird to be poking inside a trapdoor on your teacher—especially when there's nothing but wires and circuits in there.

"I see a square chip sticking out of a tiny slot," I report. "Is that it?"

The teacher nods. "Press it and it will pop out."

It's almost like the memory card of a camera. I remove it and close up Mr. Aidact's back. He takes the chip and slips it into his pants pocket.

"You have to get rid of that," Nathan reminds him.

"When the time comes," he promises, "I will."

I hand him the bus ticket to Denver. "It leaves at eleven forty-five sharp. Platform six. We saw Mr. Perkins in the parking lot with three government goons. So the minute the game ends, you've got to get out of here."

"Goons." A head tilt. "An enforcer hired to terrorize or eliminate adversaries. Yes, I suppose they are goons from my point of view."

Outside, we hear the shrill of a whistle, and Mr. Aidact hurries off to take charge of his team.

"I wish he'd let us flush that chip," Nathan tells me. "What if he forgets to get rid of it?"

"No, it's smart," I reply. "If Perkins realizes that his robot and his chip aren't together, he'll know something's up."

By the time we emerge from the field house, the bleachers are packed and kids ring the field on the sidelines. The buzz of nervous excitement is almost electric. We know it's all about Mr. Aidact's escape plan, but the Seahawks' fans probably think we're this amped about middle school field hockey. They're looking around at us like we've flipped out.

Cassidy and the Seahawks' captain square off at the centerline. Then it's game on.

And there's a lot more at stake than one little state championship.

Principal Candiotti

Some people think a principal's day ends when the buses pull out and the kids are gone. Nothing could be further from the truth. This job never ends. More often than not, dinner is a sandwich or a salad at my desk, as I struggle to get through paperwork and parent contacts. It's only been more hectic lately, with the whole community up in arms about the AIDACT project.

Well, at least that will be over soon. I take no comfort in it. I like Mr. Aidact. I suppose I should change my wording now: I *liked* Mr. Aidact. But pretty soon he'll be nothing more than a carton or two of spare parts.

Saturday morning finds me on the way to the grocery

store to pick up ingredients for another week's worth of sandwiches and salads. My weekends are almost as busy as my weeks, since I have just those two days to get all my errands done. Actually, I don't mind shopping. It's almost soothing in its simplicity—until I pass by Memorial Field.

Something big is going on there. The parking lot is full and the bleachers are jammed with people. Even with the windows up and the radio on, I can hear the cheering. I sigh wanly. That could have been us. The Bobcats were supposed to be playing on that field in the state championship that wasn't to be. It sure didn't take the Parks Department very long to find another event to host there.

And then I catch a glimpse of the action on the field and almost drive up a telephone pole. It's field hockey! And one of the teams is in teal and white!

I pull over to the side of the road and stare. Certainly, we're not the only school to wear those colors. But—I catch sight of a lone figure standing on the sidelines, ramrod straight, absolutely still, as if somebody planted a man-shaped flagpole right there. It's Mr. Aidact! It has to be! This is *our* game! Somehow, against the wishes of their parents, and ignoring everything I told them, the Bobcats are playing for their championship. Why?

School spirit? Bobcat pride? Some of that, sure. But mostly, they're doing it for *him*. Mr. Aidact. Word travels through a middle school faster than head lice—of course they figured out that he's leaving. Kids aren't burdened by the prejudices of their parents. And they came back to him one last time.

I abandon the car in a no-parking zone and run to Memorial Field, squeezing myself in among the standees on the sidelines.

A piece of paper is shoved into my hands and a young voice tells me, "When the game is over, we're all going to . . ." Then Avalon's wide eyes stare at me and the words taper off.

I examine the paper. It reads: MR. AIDACT IS UNREAL.

"He certainly is, Avalon," I tell her. "In more ways than one."

She backs away from me like she's afraid I bite. My principal-sense tingles. Something is definitely up. But the roar from the bleachers draws my attention back to the field. Rosalie sends a long pass bouncing to Cassidy, who fires it into the net. And just like that, the score is 4–3, with the Seahawks in the lead. The Bobcats are down, but they're still in this game.

And their principal is with them all the way.

Nathan Popova

It's getting really loud in the bleachers. When Cassidy scores that goal to bring Brightling within one, I jump to my feet and scream myself hoarse right along with everybody else.

It earns me an exasperated glance from Oliver. "You don't care about field hockey," he reminds me. "You barely care about sports at all."

"I know, I know," I confess in a low voice. "But you get caught up in this stuff when it's your own school."

"Keep your eye on the ball. Not *that* ball," he adds quickly. "The one that has to bounce our way when this game ends. And keep an eye on *them*." He inclines his head to the spot two rows in front of us where Perkins and the three engineers are seated.

I nod my agreement. Like this escape isn't already complicated enough, we have an extra job to do the second the game ends. In the chaotic crowd, we have to snatch the briefcase out of Perkins's hands and make sure Mr. Aidact gets it. If he's going to have a future living on his own, he's going to have to be able to make self-repairs.

"Okay, I get it," I concede. "It doesn't matter if we win or lose. So what's the harm in winning? We'll get a new trophy. Then maybe people will stop asking what happened to the *old* trophy."

Oliver looks at me like he'd love to trade me in for a smarter friend.

Oh, sure, he's right that the escape is all that matters. But I'd really love to beat these Seahawks. They've got an awful lot of swagger for a middle school team. But I have to admit they're good. Every time the Bobcats even the score, the Seahawks always come up with another goal to go one up on us. By the halftime whistle, Sheridan Middle School clings to a 6–5 lead.

As kids hop down from the bleachers to stretch their legs and head to the snack bar to warm up with hot chocolate, Oliver and I race to the field house, where the two teams have retreated to their locker rooms. There, hanging on the doorknob, is a Bobcats cap and windbreaker exactly like the team gear Mr. Aidact is wearing.

Through the door, we can hear the coach's pep talk to his players. "We have to increase our time of possession. We held the ball for forty-six percent of the first half. That's not good enough. . . ."

We roll the hat up in the jacket and deliver it to Darryl in the front row of the bleachers.

"Don't put these on until the minute the game ends," Oliver cautions.

As the tallest kid in school, Darryl's job is to impersonate Mr. Aidact when everybody rushes the field. If Perkins and the engineers are drawn by Darryl's six-foot-one frame in the jacket and hat amid the surging crowd, that might buy the escapee some precious seconds in his dash for the bus station.

"Got it," Darryl confirms, accepting the bundle. "You can count on me."

Stinky sits next to him, his eyes wide with concern. "How does Mr. Aidact seem?"

"We didn't see him," I admit. "He was giving the girls a pep talk for the second half."

Darryl shakes his head in admiration. "That guy's something else. Here he is, facing being stripped down for spare parts. But does he let it bother him?"

"You know he's a robot, right?" Stinky asks him.

"Doesn't matter," Darryl insists. "He's quality. Good coach too. How much you want to bet we win?"

Oliver peers across the field and frowns. "What's Candiotti doing here? She's not supposed to know about this game."

I experience a new alert—one that has nothing to do with Oliver. "Do you think she's figured out that we're trying to save Mr. Aidact?"

"Maybe she's just hoping for another field hockey trophy," Darryl suggests. "You know how much she loved the old one."

"Is the plan still on?" Stinky asks anxiously.

"Absolutely," Oliver replies. "But we have to keep an eye on her. It's impossible to know whose side she's on."

The second half begins with a quick goal for the Seahawks, padding their lead to two. The Bobcats fight back, throwing everything they have against their opponents from Sheridan Middle School. They dominate the play, but the Seahawks' goalie makes save after save, keeping the ball out.

I'm on the edge of my seat, and so is everybody else, willing our team to get back into the game. On the sidelines, Principal Candiotti is twisting and gyrating with an invisible stick, trying to use body English to squeeze a shot into the opposing net. With every thwarted attempt on goal, the crowd lets out a frustrated *"Awwwwww!"* Down 7–5, with time ticking away, can the Bobcats come back?

"I can't believe you don't care," I scold Oliver. "I get that we're not sports fans, but this is really intense. You're not even looking at the side of the field where the action is!"

"I've got all the action I need," he replies in a voice thick with tragedy. "Krumlich is here."

I follow his pointing finger. Sure enough, there's Kevin, wading into the crowd of standees ringing the field. Fifteen seconds later, he's got his phone out and he's punching in numbers.

"He's too late, right?" I ask, hoping to convince myself as much as Oliver. "Even if he blabs all over town and the news reaches every parent at Brightling, they still won't have time to shut down the game!"

But before ten minutes have gone by, cars begin pulling into the parking lot, disgorging Brightling parents. It starts as a trickle, yet pretty soon it's a steady flood.

"Krumlich!" Oliver rages. "He's like Paul Revere with a cell phone. The robots are coaching! The robots are coaching!"

I recognize a lot of the Bobcats' parents. Uh-oh—there's Rosalie's mother, president of the PTA. She's talking a blue streak, haranguing the other moms and dads. Then she pushes to the head of the small army and marches them through the gate.

Around the periphery comes Mrs. Candiotti, her knees pumping high as she rushes to reach the invaders. She blocks their path, arms spread wide, as if she thinks she can hold back two dozen angry people from running onto the turf. It's a standoff—principal versus parents.

"If they storm the field," Oliver murmurs, "we have to put the plan into action early."

"But the game won't be over yet," I protest. "What if Mr. Aidact won't leave?"

We stare down at the tense confrontation on the sidelines. Something has to give.

And something does. On the field, Rosalie unleashes a long, clumsy shot that bounces its way through players from both teams. Screened by the traffic, their goalie sees it too late. The ball bounces off her foot and winds up in the back of the net.

The roar of the crowd startles the avenging mob of parents. Seeing Rosalie accepting the congratulations of her teammates, Mrs. Arnette starts shrieking, "That was *my* daughter! That was Rosalie!"

It stops the invaders in their tracks. It doesn't make them any less mad. But they suddenly realize there's a championship up for grabs—and their daughters are down by only a single goal. They settle in to see if the Bobcats can pull off another miracle comeback against Sheridan Middle School. And as for the team's robot coach, they'll deal with that once the outcome has been decided.

It's nail-biting time. With only 3:53 remaining in the game, the Seahawks just have to hold on. They retreat into a defensive shell, with all eleven players inside the sixteen-yard circle. The Bobcats throw the kitchen sink at them. But with the circle so crowded, there's no room to operate. There are so many stick fouls and body bumps that the whistle blows every few seconds. The strategy is obvious—to run out the clock on meaningless stoppages of play.

The crowd—so loud just moments ago—becomes deathly quiet as the clock ticks down to the final minute. You can hear Mr. Aidact, calling to his team:

"Stay relaxed . . . don't panic . . . plenty of time . . ."

But there isn't plenty of time. Fifteen seconds, then ten, then five.

Cassidy takes a desperate swipe at the ball. It slices into the melee in front of the net, ricochets off one Seahawk's toe, bounces against another's heel, and trickles through the goalie's pads a split second before the clock turns to all zeroes. The referee raises his arms, signifying a Bobcats goal.

The Brightling fans explode in joyful celebration.

"Now!" Oliver grabs my arm and tries to drag me down the bleachers. But the row in front of us isn't budging. *Nobody's* budging. We bounce off, dazed.

Oliver is practically hysterical. "Why isn't everybody rushing the field? The game is over!"

"No, it isn't!" I hiss. "It's seven–seven!"

"So it's a tie! You think I care about that *now*?"

"It's the championship game!" I point to the field, where the umpire has pulled both teams together for a briefing. "Look—they're setting up for overtime!"

35

Oliver Zahn

"Overtime?" I pull my phone out of my pocket and check the screen. It's 11:31! "We can't do overtime! That bus is leaving in *fourteen minutes!*"

"We have to," Nathan insists. "You know Mr. Aidact won't abandon the team. You think he's going to bail on them when they're so close?"

"But he's got a bus to catch!" My voice is coming out high and panicky—like a little kid who's lost at the mall. "If he has to stand around the depot, waiting for the next bus, Perkins and the engineers are going to find him and shut him down!"

"Shhh!" Nathan's eyes are on the group from the

Department of Education, sitting just two rows in front of us. "It's not going to work out so great if *they* hear you," he adds in a low voice.

Down on the field, sudden-death overtime begins. But up in the bleachers, I'm in agony because this could be *real* sudden death for Mr. Aidact if our plans go down the drain. What's a rule-wrecker to do? It's going to take split-second timing and perfect execution to get him away from those engineers. But if he misses the bus, thanks to *overtime*—no amount of preparation can save you from that.

I sit there, fuming and freaking, while precious minutes slip away. I can't even watch the game. "*Somebody score!*" I shout in exasperation. Honestly, I don't care who wins, so long as it happens *now*.

"Don't say that!" Nathan pleads. "How can we make it this far only to lose in overtime?"

I see his point. After dominating during the comeback, the Bobcats have run out of gas, and Leticia is in a shooting gallery.

Come on, Seahawks—score! Get it over with!

"Mr. Aidact has to do something!" Nathan laments. "Otherwise we'll lose for sure!"

At that very instant, a whistle stops the play, and the Bobcats' coach runs out to talk to the umpire. Pretty soon, there's an animated conference underway, involving most of the two teams.

"Oh, great," I mutter savagely. "Now we can waste even more time *talking*." The bus leaves for Denver in only *nine minutes!*

Mr. Aidact keeps pointing at the Seahawks' goalie. And the next thing you know, the umpire gets out a yardstick and measures her pads.

"Could this take any longer?" I seethe. "I don't care if those things are fifteen feet wide! Get on with it!"

"No, this is *good!*" Nathan exclaims excitedly. "If the pads are too big, it's a foul."

"I don't care if it's a crime against humanity!"

The umpire signals a penalty stroke—a free shot on goal. My mind races. If we end the game right here, right now, there still might be time to make it to the bus.

We have to wait for their goalie to change into legal pads, while the Sheridan parents complain bitterly, and our fans shout them down.

This is no penalty corner. It's a shot from directly in front of the net. Captain Cassidy stands over the ball as Memorial Field becomes deathly quiet.

Suddenly, I'm the biggest Bobcats fan in the whole place. *Don't miss!* I exhort, beaming mental energy from my brain to hers.

Cassidy pulls back her stick to blast the ball into the top left-hand corner. Then, just as the goalie commits, she flicks her wrists and sends a modest little dribbler into the opposite side of the net.

Final score: 8–7 for the new state-champions, the Brightling Bobcats.

I absolutely did not care who won this game. I believe school spirit is a plot cooked up by teachers to keep kids from wrecking rules. But I have to admit I like the sound of that.

A scream of celebration erupts from every Brightling throat. The Bobcats mob their coach. That's step one of the plan—but for sure, they would have mobbed him anyway. Without his electronic eyes to notice the illegal pads, who knows how this game might have ended? It was his final contribution to this miracle season.

The rumble of hundreds of feet running down the metal stands is like a stampede of thundering buffalo. Nathan and I are right with them. As we come up behind Perkins and the three engineers, I reach out, snatch the giant briefcase by its handle, and carry it away with me.

I hear a loud *"Hey!"* from behind, but I'm already too far down the bleachers for anybody to grab me. Up ahead, kids are pouring onto the field, converging on the winning team and, at their center, the victorious coach.

As we hit the grass, Darryl's waiting for us, clutching the jacket and hat that will turn him into our Mr. Aidact look-alike.

I grab him by the arm. "Come with us!" We begin to wade into the boiling mob that surrounds the celebrating state champs. Everybody's bouncing up and down, which isn't so easy when you're carrying a heavy briefcase.

Out of the corner of my eye, I spy Perkins and the engineers charging toward the crowd. With my free hand, I rip the MR. AIDACT IS UNREAL flyer out of Stinky's hand and throw it straight up. That's the signal for everybody to do the same. In seconds, the air is white with a blizzard of Avalon's flyers.

Nathan and Darryl get behind me, and—using the briefcase as a plow—I blast my way to the center of the celebration. I don't know if dancing was ever part of Mr. Aidact's original programming, but he's doing it now, right along with the girls, leading them in a rousing chorus of "We Are the Champions." You get the sense that he could be a rock star if he put his AI to it.

"Pupils!" he greets us. "We won! How dope is this?"

"You remember you're leaving, right?" I shout over the noise.

"Indubitably."

"Already?" Rosalie is crushed. "Can't we keep him just a little longer?"

I toss my head in the direction of Perkins and the engineers, who are approaching the edge of the mob. "The bus leaves in five minutes!" I hiss. "It's now or never!"

Mr. Aidact rips off his teal hat and jacket, and I stuff the heavy briefcase into his arms.

"*Signs!*" I bellow.

All at once, a double row of huge posters is unrolling in front of us, creating a clear pathway out of the crush of people. Mr. Aidact dashes down his escape route, Nathan and I hot on his heels. A backward glance shows me that Darryl, now dressed in teal, is at the center of the partying Bobcats. A split second later, Perkins and the engineers break through to him. It takes them a long moment to realize who he is—and, more important, who he isn't.

Perkins catches a fleeting glimpse of his AIDACT unit sprinting for freedom. But before he can react, the sign holders collapse the escape route, trapping the engineers in the middle of the crowd.

By this time Mr. Aidact is at full gallop. He hurdles the fence surrounding the field and barrels down the sidewalk, dodging pedestrians. Nathan and I are running our fastest, but we're falling behind.

"It's platform six!" I holler, hoping my voice will reach him. "Platform six!"

Without turning around, he raises the briefcase like it weighs nothing and waves it in our direction.

I catch sight of the clock in front of the bank: 11:42. The bus leaves in *three minutes!*

"Oh no!" Nathan wheels and points. The Department of Education cube van is pulling out of the Memorial Field parking lot. "Mr. Aidact is fast, but he can't outrun a truck!"

The fleeing robot is way ahead of us, but he's still got a block and a half to go before he reaches the depot.

Just as the van is about to pull into traffic, a navy blue sedan squeals around the corner and screeches to a halt, blocking the driveway. The van lurches to a stop, inches from a collision.

Nathan and I instantly recognize the driver of the car. "Mrs. Candiotti!" we chorus.

The engineers lean on the horn, but the principal won't budge.

As Mr. Aidact approaches the depot, a bus turns out and heads for the highway.

"No!" I wail, all the energy suddenly draining out of me. "He missed it!"

That's when I see the sign over the windshield:

MIAMI. There's still hope. The Denver bus hasn't left yet.

When Mr. Aidact disappears into the building, the station clock reads 11:44. The Denver bus is set to depart in *one minute*. He *has* to be on it.

Please let him be on it!

Nathan and I pull out all the stops and race into the building. Platform six is directly in front of us. And—hooray—the Denver bus is still there! But—

"Where's Mr. Aidact?" Nathan pants.

We look around desperately. There he is at platform five, where the bus to New York is loading up luggage. As we watch, Mr. Aidact reaches into his pocket, pulls out the GPS chip, and tosses it into the baggage compartment.

Brilliant. When they search for the tracker, it will be on its way to New York. I couldn't have planned it better myself.

There's an abrupt hiss and the door of the Denver bus starts to close.

Pure panic seizes me. What could be worse than missing it when he's *right here*?

Nathan and I lunge into the opening to keep the door from closing. It hurts, but I've never been so happy to get crushed by something.

"Mister—wait!" Nathan rasps in a strained voice. "Our—uh—uncle is coming!"

The driver is impatient. "Tell him to hurry up. I've got a schedule to keep."

"Uncle Aidact!" I call. "Come quick! Your bus is leaving!"

In an instant, he's directly in front of us, one foot on the bus's bottom step.

Relief floods over me. He made it. But just as quickly, it dawns on me that this is goodbye. We're never going to lay eyes on our new teacher again. I feel a lump in my throat the size of a bowling ball. All at once, it doesn't seem so long ago that I was mad at him because he caught that spitball on the very first day of school.

But there's no time to say any of that. The driver is looking at his watch and glaring at us.

So I just blurt, "We'll never forget you."

"And I'll never forget you," he replies. "Unless I stand too close to a strong magnet. Goodbye, pupils. Aidact out."

We stand there, practically at attention, as the door closes and the bus pulls away. I'm afraid to say anything for fear that my voice might crack.

Nathan swallows hard. "I wonder who our new homeroom teacher is going to be."

"Doesn't matter," I tell him. "Whoever it is won't be as good."

Walking out of the depot into the cold sunshine is like entering a strange new world—one where Brightling is a state champion and Mr. Aidact doesn't teach there anymore.

"Oliver—" Nathan squeezes my shoulder.

I stare. The Department of Education cube van is idling right in front of the station. One of the engineers is at the wheel. Beside him, in the passenger seat, Perkins pounds the keyboard of a laptop computer.

"They're tracking him," I whisper.

At that moment, two buses drive up to the depot exit and pause at the street. The Denver bus waits to make a left turn, while the New York bus continues straight down the avenue.

Barely daring to breath, Nathan and I watch as the cube van makes an awkward U-turn, cutting off the Denver bus, and speeds away after the vehicle headed to New York. I picture the GPS chip in the baggage compartment, sending its signal to Perkins's computer.

The Denver bus finally makes its left turn. As it passes, we can see Mr. Aidact in a window seat near the front. His head is thrown back and he's laughing.

It's like a great weight has been lifted off my shoulders. "He's going to be okay!"

Nathan is nervous. "How do you figure that?"

"He's *laughing!*" I crow. "Don't you get it? He sent those engineers on a wild-goose chase, and his AI taught him how funny that is. *He finally has a sense of humor!*"

"It *is* pretty funny," he concedes. "Especially if they follow that bus all the way to New York."

"Way to go, Mr. Aidact!" I applaud. "With artificial intelligence *and* a sense of humor, he's unstoppable!"

CONFIDENTIAL REPORT

To: Department of Education, Washington, DC
From: Paul Perkins, PE
Project: AIDACT

While it's never good news when a $250 million project has to be scrapped, and a valuable piece of equipment goes missing, I don't think the AIDACT experiment should be considered a total failure. Never before in the history of artificial intelligence has a robot conspired with middle school students to act against all its programming and thwart the plans its designers had for it. The fact that this AIDACT unit actually succeeded in its escape proves that its AI capabilities are far more sophisticated than anything we could have imagined. It will add a great deal to our knowledge to examine the AI system if and when we ever find the unit, which seems unlikely. By the time the engineering team caught up to the bus on the New Jersey Turnpike and realized AIDACT wasn't on it, the unit could have been almost anywhere in the continental US and Canada.

PROJECT STATUS: On Hold

SPECIAL EXPENSES

1 engineering toolkit

Gas reimbursement (14.5 gallons)

1 package extra-strength carsickness remedy

Rosalie Arnette

The new field hockey trophy goes right on the empty pedestal where the old field hockey trophy used to stand.

I know I only tried out for the team because it would look good on my student record. But I'm really proud of it. Any way you slice it, a state championship is a humongous achievement. And however proud the players are, multiply that by fifty thousand and you've got Principal Candiotti.

Seriously, ever since the game, she's been smiling so wide that it looks like her face is about to crack. Even when the grease trap caught fire in the kitchen and smoked out the whole cafeteria, she couldn't work up much of a frown for the fire department when they arrived. It's that kind of happy.

The first time we see our trophy is the morning Mrs. Candiotti invites all the Bobcats into her office before homeroom. We drink sparkling apple cider out of plastic champagne glasses and toast our glorious victory.

The principal holds her glass high. "From one Bobcat to you others, across the generations!"

We all drink, and Cassidy adds, "And to Coach Aidact. We'd give it all back if you could still be here with us."

That gets a big cheer, and we clink glasses, even though plastic doesn't clink. We all start chattering about how awesome the escape was and how Mr. Aidact made the entire Department of Education look like a bunch of clowns. We talk about what a fantastic coach he was—how nice, how smart—and how he inspired us and turned us into a true team. He didn't abandon us when we abandoned him, not even when he was putting himself at risk by sticking around. I hear words like *great guy*, *super-coach*, *mentor*, *genius*, and *friend*. The one word I don't hear is *robot*. Mr. Aidact has always been as real to us as our own families.

"Now, girls," Mrs. Candiotti chides. "What took place after the game should never have happened, and it cost our government an awful lot of money. I hope none of you were involved."

She has to say that. She's a principal, so the Department of Education is sort of her boss. But I can see a traffic violation sitting open on her desk. It's dated the day of the game, and the charge is for blocking the parking lot exit at Memorial Field. We all saw her. She may complain about the escape, but she helped it along as much as anybody—maybe even as much as Oliver and Nathan.

In the awkward silence, I look out the window at her panoramic view of the Brightling Ravine. I guess it makes sense that the best view in the whole school should go to the principal. Maybe I'll be a principal one day, with an office just like this one—big windows, amazing view. It's possible, you know. With a state championship on my record, I could get into any college and achieve anything.

It's a great celebration, but pretty soon the bell rings, calling us all to homeroom. As I file out behind the other girls, I stub my toe on a small cardboard box at the doorway. Looking down, I'm surprised to see the *old* field hockey trophy, broken into pieces.

"You found it!" I exclaim.

"Someone returned it—what's left of it," Mrs. Candiotti confirms. "It was in a plastic bag, hanging on the doorknob of the gym entrance. No note. Just the pieces."

"Are you going to have it fixed?" I ask. "This is *your* state championship, just like we have ours."

The principal shakes her head. "I don't live in the past. You girls are the stars now. Enjoy this moment."

✳

On the way to homeroom, I'm surprised to run into Mr. Perkins coming out of the faculty lounge. No one's seen him since the championship game.

I always thought he was kind of a jerk, but I'm a little bit sorry for him now. He's carrying a carton with an assortment of books and papers, and he looks a lot like a guy in a TV show who got fired and had to clean out his desk.

He fixes me with an expression I can't quite identify. Regret? Disappointment? Anger?

I swallow hard. "I'm sorry about—what happened. I hope you didn't get in too much trouble." I indicate the box in his arms.

"I didn't lose my job, if that's what you mean," he replies stiffly. "My role here was always attached to the AIDACT unit. Now that the unit is no longer in the picture . . ."

I can't help smiling. The thought of Mr. Aidact's

clean getaway fills me with a glow that no state championship ever could.

I have to ask. "Do you think he can make it? You know—on his own?"

Mr. Perkins nods slowly. "Every time I felt the unit had reached the limits of its capabilities, the AI always proved me wrong. It's a very impressive technology."

"Mr. Aidact isn't technology," I tell him. "He's a person—one of the best people. And as long as you think of him as wires and circuits, you're never going to understand him."

I start to move on, but he stops me. "Wait. One question—did he get the toolkit?"

"He did," I confirm.

"Good," Mr. Perkins says slowly. "There are always minor repairs and adjustments."

I stare at him. Maybe our "student teacher" has a heart after all.

✳

Our new homeroom teacher is Ms. Van Dyke, and we know she's not a robot because she has a cold. She's been sneezing and blowing for the past week. Also, she doesn't have some guy pretending to be a student teacher, toting a giant briefcase and following her around.

Oliver is determined to get her to call us "pupils." He's constantly asking questions like, "Can a pupil use the bathroom anytime we want, or do we pupils have to get a hall pass?" Or "What were the pupils like in your old school? Were the pupils there any different than the pupils here?"

So far, she's still calling us "students" and "class." But knowing Oliver, he'll break her down.

"How was the Bobcats thing in Candiotti's office?" Nathan whispers.

"Pretty good," I reply. "But you'll never guess what I saw. Remember the *old* trophy—the one that got stolen? Well, somebody brought it back, busted into pieces!"

Nathan goes bright red. "The high school kids!" he blurts.

"What high school kids?"

Oliver elbows him in the ribs to keep him quiet.

Okay, that explains a lot. Of course they were involved in what happened to that old trophy. Most of the unexplained disasters at this school involve those two.

But lately, I've been finding it harder and harder to stay mad at Nathan and Oliver. I think it's because they did so much to help Mr. Aidact escape. I'll always be grateful to them for that.

I wonder where he is and how he's doing. I hope he's happy, even though Mr. Perkins doesn't think a machine can know what happy is.

What if the Department of Education tracks him down? What if he blows a circuit or runs into a software glitch he can't fix? There are a million things that can go wrong. And the hardest part is that we'll never know.

Epilogue

NATIONAL FIELD HOCKEY CHAMPIONSHIP GOES TO SMALL SCHOOL

ROCKY MOUNTAIN NEWS: It's the ultimate Cinderella story. Tiny McLaren Academy, an all-girls school with fewer than a hundred students, has won the National Girls' Middle School Field Hockey Championship, defeating teams from schools fifteen and even twenty times its size. How did a small-town institution that didn't even have an athletic program a year ago rise to the very pinnacle of middle school sports?

"My pupils deserve all the credit," said McLaren's new coach, a young teacher named Nathan Oliver. . . .

Books by
GORDON KORMAN

THE MASTERMINDS SERIES

BALZER + BRAY

An Imprint of HarperCollinsPublishers

harpercollinschildrens.com